He Loves Me,

He Loves You Not 2

Puppetmaster

A Novel by

Mychea

GOOD2GO PUBLISHING

Published by:
GOOD2GO PUBLISHING
7311 W. Glass Lane
Laveen, AZ 85339
www.good2gopublishing.com
Twitter @good2gobooks
G2G@good2gopublishing.com
Facebook.com/good2gopublishing
ThirdLane Marketing: Brian James
Brian@good2gopublishing.com

Cover design: Davida Baldwin
Typesetter: Hariett Wilson
ISBN: 978-098918590

Acknowledgments

Dedicated to my goddaughter Jasmine Nicole Woodyear.
Your god mommy absolutely loves and adores you.

Me'Shell Stewart (My MeMe) words cannot begin to express my gratitude to the powers that be that introduced us all those years ago in kindergarten. You have truly been a blessing to me in more ways than one and I am so thankful for you. PS: Thanks for the synopsis help. It was greatly appreciated! Love you! ~M~

Silk White, you already know….

I want to say thank you to all my fans, you all are the reason that I continue to do what I do. To the ones that have been holding me down since my very first book Coveted hit the street and I was hand delivering them thank you so much for having faith in me then and continuing to believe in me now to supply you with enough drama and entertainment you cannot put a Mychea novel down. There are some fans that truly go above and beyond measure and I am completely grateful to them. They come to casting calls or stop by signings if I'm in their area just to say hello and I am forever in your debt. The amount of love is contagious and I love you all back. Shout out to some pretty amazing fans of mine Leandra Baker, Ashley Varnes and Brian Christian you all totally rock out!

Email: mycheawrites@yahoo.com   Website: www.mychea.com

Time is ticking,
as it's ticking;
I am sitting,
as I am sitting;
they feel safer,
as they feel safer;
I am plotting;
as Iam plotting
I am waiting,
as I am waiting
days are passing;
as days are passing
they're forgetting;
as they're forgetting
I grow stronger;
as I grow stronger
they will see....

...revenge truly is the sweetest joy.

Having just returned from the sunny and relaxing atmosphere of Miami's south beach, she thought this weather was certainly a temperature shock taking in the crisp breeze from the autumn air, her almond shaped brown eyes reflecting disgust behind her oversized cream Gucci sunglasses that rested on her nose. She was watching the happy family playing tag in the park; who were oblivious to the fact that they were the center of attention by an attractive young woman sitting at the Starbucks across from the park, drinking a caramel apple spice, she observed them on their family outing calculating her next move. She hoped that they enjoyed today because it would be the last peaceful day she allowed them to have…

Chapter 1

As the heavy steel door sealed in place and locked behind him, Trent began to have second thoughts about what he was about to do. Walking down the long hallway, he took in the cold, isolating feel of the building and wondered how people could survive in a dark, unwelcome place such as this.

Approaching another steel door, Trent waited patiently to be buzzed through the door into the visiting room. Entering the visiting room, Trent sat in the chair facing the wire cage taking in his surroundings as he waited for the person he was visiting to appear on the opposite side of the cage.

Watching as she came to sit in the seat at the opposite side of the wire cage, Trent couldn't help but notice how much she had changed in appearance. Her once full head of hair was lying flat against her head with no life to it. Her brown eyes, once so full of animation and love lost their luster. She was no longer the attractive sex kitten whom she used to be.

"Hey."

"Why are you here?" Trent flinched at her tone. If anyone should be upset, it should be him, not the other way around.

"I wanted to check on you."

"Why?" She shrugged with dull eyes. "I tried to kill you. Why would you check on me?"

"Because," Trent hesitated before continuing. "I understand why you did what you did. As messed up as it is, I understand and I forgive you."

Phylicia's smile transformed her entire face. She lit up from the inside out. This was her first real smile in over three years. Tears flashed in her eyes. She knew what she had done was wrong, but Trent must really love her to come and visit her at her worse.

"Thank you," she whispered and her heart smiled. She knew that Trent loved her, his visit proved it.

"You're welcome." Trent said watching as she tried to hide the tears. "How are you holding up in here?"

"How do you think?" She retorted with a lack of enthusiasm. "I'm alive if that's what you mean." Phylicia shrugged her shoulders as she averted her eyes from his calm, patient ones. Her life was in serious chaos. She had been disbarred from practicing law. Her daughter Avionne had been placed in foster care and wasn't allowed to visit her. She hadn't been outside the asylum grounds in over three years. She'd forgotten what the real world was like.

"Why do you forgive me?" Phylicia inquired. "I killed our daughter." The tears that she had held back, slowly streamed down her malnourished face.

"I can't even forgive myself for that," she gazed off into space remembering. "I laced her food with rat poison for over a month. That's why she stayed sick so much. That weekend she was at your place, I knew that would be her final weekend. All the food I sent with her was heavily dosed with the poison. I knew she wouldn't survive." Swallowing audibly Phylicia continued, while shaking her head.

"What kind of mother kills her baby in the hopes that it will bring the man she once loved back to her and make them closer?" Trent asked her in hurt and disgust. Khloe had been his daughter too, and he missed her. If it weren't for Phylicia, she would be alive today. Trent watched Phylicia as she waged an eternal war within herself that he couldn't help her fight. Most people wouldn't understand why he felt it necessary to forgive Phylicia and visit her to see how she was doing. But he felt like all of this was his fault and he owed her that because being in love with him had driven her to the breaking point of insanity, so he felt partly to blame.

"I miss Khloe, too." Trent shifted his eyes from Phylicia. He'd had to pray many days to God about Phylicia killing his baby girl. It had taken three long years and counseling, which had finally brought him here today to face Phylicia and let her know that she was forgiven. He had forgiven her.

"I forgive you because God has worked with me. You need to pray so He can help you forgive you."

"I don't know if I'm with all that. How is the wife?" Phylicia said, wiping her eyes and abruptly changing the subject.

Trent eyed Phylicia warily.

"She's good. Thanks for asking."

Phylicia snorted, "Sad to see that's still going on."

Trent shook his head in disbelief at her audacity. "Yo, P, don't start. She's my wife. Of course it's still going. It will be 'going on' forever."

"We'll see about that." Phylicia said with malice in her tone.

Trent shook his head; he wasn't in the mood to deal with Phylicia's antics and subliminal threats. "Just when I thought it was safe to come see you because time may have matured you." Trent stood in disgust, "I see that nothing has changed."

Phylicia glanced up at him with a smug look on her face. "You came because you still love me. It's okay to admit it."

Trent looked down at Phylicia sadly. She would never change. He had come here hoping to see that person that he had once fallen in love with. The woman whom he had wanted to spend the rest of his life with at one time, the woman who had consumed his whole being, whom he'd, wanted to protect and make love to daily. Now he saw that he would have to accept what was, the woman who he remembered was gone and more than likely would never return.

"You will never change. I won't visit again, for my sanity. I had to see you to know that I truly had forgiven you," he stared into her brown eyes long and hard, "And I have." Trent walked away after that statement never looking back. Phylicia was in his past. He now focused   on   his   future.

THE
PAST

"No one expects to find the love of their life at twenty, or maybe some do. I was not one of those people. I wasn't a believer, until I saw him. He turned my world upside down, inside out; completely captivated me, made me yearn for him, had to fulfill myself with him. He was a thirst that I couldn't quench, a fire that couldn't be dowsed. And, for one moment in time, I was his and he was mine. Nothing in my world or his can ever take that away from us. For now until forever, he will be the one I wanted, but wasn't able to have."

~ Natalia Richele Bynes

Chapter 2

The Beginning
Friday, April 26, 1999 –Nightclub in Downtown New York

"Can you believe there is no parking…geez. For this to be the Big Apple, I am going to need them to do something about the parking situation here. This is ridiculous."

"Erikka, you know parking is what it is. It will never change. City life is city life and this is New York. Parking is now and will always be a challenge." Natalia said.

"I mean, I know but," she paused as she bucked a U-turn in the middle of the street to take the parking spot that had just freed up on the corner, "Leaving my car for the local crackhead to monitor its safety does not excite me very much."

Natalia muffled a laugh as right at that moment a fellow, she wouldn't say crack head, but he may have portrayed one just a little; walked up to Erikka's window and offered to watch her car for five dollars. Erikka cut her eyes at Natalia and through pursed lips whispered, "See, this is exactly what I be talking about," she said in disgust.

Natalia couldn't help but laugh then, "Girl, you can valet park. That is always an option you know?"

"Valet park for twenty dollars and then spend another twenty dollars on drinks and stuff inside the club? No thank you. This street parking will have to work out." Natalia continued to laugh because she understood; New York will hit you in your head price wise when you're trying to get your party on.

Once they had settled their parking situation and were inside, Natalia glanced around at all the people; the club was definitely on and poppin'. They were in the midst of some hot men. It was great. She was probably one of the youngest women in the club,

8

at eighteen; she definitely was not supposed to be at a party for the twenty-one and over. Yet, here she was.

Natalia, Erikka, and Shay were out for the night. They didn't hang out that often, but Natalia's friend Misty was dating a sports agent and could get tickets to the party, so she hollered at the girls to see if they wanted to roll and that is how they ended up here at the club on this particular night.

"I love this." Shay yelled to Natalia over the music. She was in the corner dancing with some guy. Natalia smiled at her as she turned and almost collided with Deon, the agent Misty was dating. I had never met him before, but Misty had described him to a T. Big, almost like music manager Vincent Herbert, tall and handsome with a smile that could light up a room and a presence that commanded attention.

"Is your name Natalia?" He asked her.

"Depends, are you Deon?"

"Hey baby," he said as he infolded Natalia into a hug. She hugged him back smiling, how could she resist. He was very charming in person. Whenever they had spoken on the phone, through Misty's encouragement, he had always called her 'baby'.

Pulling back, "How did you know who I was?" she asked him.

"Because you look exactly like Misty said you would," he pulled on Natalia's hat, "She told me that you would have on this big black floppy J-Lo hat. And, since no one else in the club has on a hat like this but you, it narrowed the options down for me."

Natalia laughed, "I guess you have a point there. So the party is hot. You should introduce me to someone, me and my girls are just over here just chillin'."

Deon looked Natalia up and down taking in her appearance. "I got just the person I want you to meet. I'll be back." Then he took off across the club.

Walking back over to the area where Erikka and Shay were; Natalia sat on top of a nearby table and watched them as they got their dance on. They looked like they were having a good time. While, glancing around the club everyone seemed to be having a good time. The club setting wasn't really her scene. She hated so many people being in one spot, taking up her space, and having people touch her because the club was so crowded. She wasn't fond of the extra loud music or people smoking, so she stayed seated, bopping her head to the music.

He appeared out of nowhere, grabbed Natalia's hand, bent down on one knee, and asked, "Will you marry me?"

Natalia smiled, and then began to laugh, "Umm, you don't have a ring."

He let Natalia's hand go to take off his Syracuse championship ring and slid it on her little finger. Natalia laughed as the ring slid down her finger with ease and if she did any sudden movements, would fall off without hesitation. "What about now?"

Looking at the ring and back down at him, she couldn't resist laughing again "I would love to."

He stood up and then stuck out his hand, "I would love to know the name of the woman who I am going to marry."

Grinning from ear to ear, she took his hand, "I'm Natalia, and you are?"

"I'm Trent."

With him now standing up, she could see that he had to be easily six feet tall. Trent had individual braids in his hair with a hat on his head twisted to the back. He looked like a very sexy younger version of Shemar Moore. He was wearing a white T-shirt and jeans. What got Natalia's attention was the body underneath the clothes. She knew that it was serious business when the ripples of muscle underneath a shirt can be seen. She wanted to run her hands down his entire body, but opted for his arms instead.

Reaching out, Natalia laid her hand on his forearm and slowly began to rub it up and down. Before he could say anything to her about the rubbing, his friend, whom he introduced as Tizzy, walked up and engaged him in conversation for awhile, so Natalia was free to rub on him to her heart's content.

"So, you just gonna rub me up and down in the middle of the club huh?"

Looking up into his mesmerizing, chestnut-brown eyes that crinkled at the corner as he smiled, she couldn't resist smiling to herself as she ducked her head down and removed her hand from his arm.

"My bad, I didn't realize I was still doing it."

"It's all good. My future wife can do whatever she wants."

"Oh, speaking of which," Natalia took his ring off her finger, "Here's your ring. I don't want you to forget, or I forget and go home with it."

"Why don't you hold on to it, so I have a reason to see you again?"

"I think not. You don't need to use the ring as a reason to see me again."

Gently taking the ring from my hand, he slid it back on his finger.

"Well, why don't you take my number?"

Natalia opened her purse to get her phone and realized that she had left it in the car. Lifting her head back up to look at him, "Do you mind writing your number down for me? I left my cell in the car." Giving her an incredulous look, he reached into his pocket and pulled out his cell.

"Why don't you put your number in my phone and I'll call you."

"Ok." After saving her name and number in his phone, Natalia handed it back to him.

"Do you want to dance?"

He smirked and gave a slight laugh, "I don't know how to dance."

"That's OK; all you have to do is stand there. I will take care of the rest." Natalia told him as she got in front of him and began grinding on him nice and slow, their bodies swaying harmoniously to the beat the DJ was playing.

Chapter 3

W hy didn't you tell me who you were?" Trent asked her.
Now in the broad light of day without the presence of
alcohol he had managed to figure out who Natalia was. He
hadn't seen her in years, so he hadn't been able to recognize her
when they'd met at the club as adults.

Natalia sheepishly looked away. "I didn't want you to remember me like that."

Trent eyed her incredulously. "In what way? We were all little kids back then. I just put two and two together. You've grown into a beautiful woman," he, Natalia, and Kodi had all grown up on the same block. Natalia was a few years younger than they were, but she would come around from time to time.

Natalia blushed as she took him in. The body of this man could tempt a saint. There were no if's, and's, or but's about this one. She wanted him, point blank. Natalia felt her body reacting in places she was unaware it could react. No other man who she'd dealt with in the past made her feel that way.

Natalia didn't know where to begin. The muscles that she was rubbing in the ill-lit club were much more pronounced as the sunlight from the window caressed every chiseled inch of him. She could imagine his strong arms tossing her up and flipping her over, his body gliding over hers as softly as a wave washing over a seashell. Gazing up at him, there was no denying it, she wanted this man.

"You like what you see?" Trent's amused voice broke her thoughts. He caught her first-hand staring at him. Did she like what she saw? Hell yeah she liked what she saw, and by the gleam in his eyes, he knew it. Which was why he was standing there watching her in amusement.

Leaning her head down, Natalia smiled as she blushed.

"I didn't know you were watching me watch you."

"You didn't answer the question." Tipping her head so her eyes could meet his, she felt her blush deepening. Falling prey to the hypnotic magic of his stare, Natalia knew Trent had her under his spell and she wasn't going anywhere.

"I love what I see. You've changed over the years." Gently biting the side of her lip, Natalia couldn't help it as her gaze shifted to his lips, which parted as he chuckled at her and displayed a pretty set of white teeth with a slight gap that only enhanced his sexiness.

"Are you ready to go?" He asked, removing his hand from her face and reaching for her arm. They were in his dorm room and he was taking her to lunch.

"I'm all yours. Lead me wherever you want me to go."

"Don't say that because you'll end up kidnapped somewhere."

"With you," Natalia said cutting her eyes at him, "That might not be such a bad thing."

"Don't start nothing, won't be nothing." Trent smirked. When she smiled back showcasing her Lauren London-like dimples, Trent quickly changed the subject before he was caught up in her smile.

"When did you start attending Syracuse?"

"The beginning of last semester. I needed a change of scenery from the city for a while, so I was happy to graduate Catherine McAuley High School and keep it moving. By coming out here, it offers me a rural feel and then when I'm ready for city life, it's only about four hours away." Natalia told him.

"I'm happy you came. Too bad, it took you so long to find me. I'll be graduating in a few days and relocating back to the city."

"So, what does that mean?"

"It means that we won't even get anything started. I would never do that to you."

Natalia felt as if someone had gut-punched her. She'd had a crush on Trent since they were children and now that the time had finally arrived that she was old enough to date him, he wasn't going to give her the opportunity.

"What is it you think that you'd be doing to me exactly?" Natalia whispered as she reached out her arms to pull Trent in close.

"You need to be more concerned with what I would do to you," she said pulling his head down to meet hers. Touching her lips lightly to his, testing him to see if he would kiss her back. When Trent seemed reluctant to participate, Natalia deepened the kiss, willing him to give in to her. When his arms came up around her and began to caress her back, she knew that she had him. Natalia allowed herself to relax her mind and be caught up in Trent's mouth touching hers. Melting into him, she let out a light moan when he pulled her body against his, forcing her to feel the full-length of him. Every inch of his hardness enticing her softness. Natalia was in heaven. This was what dreams were made of.

Trent abruptly jerked away from Natalia, gently pushing her away from him.

"What's wrong?" Natalia's sexually charged whisper broke the silence as she put her fingers to her swollen lips, "What have I done wrong?" Feeling a sense of rejection.

"Nothing. You've done nothing wrong." Trent said, "This is my fault."

"Why does it have to be anyone's fault? Why can't we just enjoy one another's company? We're two consenting adults."

Trent looked into Natalia's eyes and knew that she was genuinely interested in him, but he didn't know where he stood about the whole thing. She was an old childhood friend and he was moving back to the city. Their timing was off. He was about to begin a completely new life now that he had graduated and wasn't really interested in dealing with someone who was still in school.

Natalia could see the inner struggle in Trent, giving him a shy smile that highlighted her deep dimples. Feeling very bold and take charge, she wanted to persuade this situation to go her way. Removing her shirt as she closed the narrow distance between them, she grabbed his hand and let her shirt fall to the floor. Keeping his hand locked under hers, she moved it to her collarbone and let their fingers linger there. Natalia's eyes were locked on Trent's and she sighed with satisfaction as his eyes began to cloud with desire. Excited about this small victory, she gingerly trailed their fingers down from her collarbone to the curve of her breast and allowed him to feel the complete swell of her breast.

Trent knew deep down that he shouldn't get involved with Natalia, especially with him graduating in a few days and moving on with his life away from this place, but he couldn't lie to himself. He was attracted to her.

Eyeing her as she watched for his reaction as she ran his hands over her breast, Trent knew there would be no turning back. He wanted her, so have her, he must. Pulling his hand away from hers and catching her by the waist, he pulled her in for another kiss. This time he deepened the kiss as he unhooked her pink and white lace bra. Moving her to his bed as he continued to kiss her, Trent scooped Natalia into his arms and gently placed her on his twin-sized mattress, only breaking their kiss to remove his clothes. He looked down at her body, which was nude from head to waist and observed as her young perky breasts rose and fell with each breath she took and then gazed long and hard into her deep brown eyes.

"Are you sure that this is something that you want to do? Once it is done, there's no coming back from it." Trent said continuing to watch her as he moved his hand to the top button of her jeans.

"I want this. I want you." Natalia replied lifting her hand up softly to caress his face. "Please," she whispered before biting her lip, closing her eyes, and lifting her hips slightly to make it easier for him to remove her jeans.

Satisfied with her answer, Trent removed her jeans and panties then lowered his head and let his mouth follow the trail his fingers had just been only moments before since she wanted this he was going to give her the night of her life.

Chapter 4

❝Hi boo!" Natalia smiled as Trent opened the door.

Natalia was living on cloud nine. She knew Trent was still going back and forth about being involved with her, but she did her best not to dwell on those little details.

Trent gave her a slight smile.

"What's up?' He bent down and gave her a gentle kiss on the cheek.

"Nothing. I came to check on you to see how your move was coming and offer you a hand if I could."

Trent gave her a hesitant smile. "I'm good, but I could use the company if you want to chill with me for a little while."

"Cool. You sure you don't need help? I got two hands that I can put to use."

Trent smiled at her statement as he loaded the last of his things into boxes.

"Nah, shortie. I got it." Trent looked over at her sitting Indian-style on his bed. "What you going to do once I'm out?" You coming back to the city for the summer?"

Natalia gazed deep into his eyes.

"I don't know. That depends on you."

Trent paused to lift his box off the floor and looked back over at her.

"What does you going home for the summer have to do with me?"

"Everything." Natalia looked at him in bewilderment, "Don't you know how I feel about you?"

"Aye, I thought we talked about this the first night we hooked up. I told you that I'm about to be out of this place and didn't want to get anything serious started. Thought we were just kicking it til' I left?"

Natalia smiled pearly whites at him. "Well, it all depends on if you want to see me or not because I've transferred to NYU, so

I'll be in the city with you." Natalia uncrossed her legs and stood up to merge the distance between her and Trent. "See, so we can make this work if you want it to."

Trent sat down on his bare mattress and sighed. He hadn't been looking to get involved with anyone. He had just graduated the day before, finished school, and wanted to be free from everything. He didn't want to crush her feelings, but he wasn't really feeling her like that.

"I'm not really looking for a relationship. You should have stayed enrolled in school here. We don't have a future, at least not right now." Trent was amazed that Natalia would take things this far by transferring schools when he thought they were just having fun until she left.

Natalia stared at him long and hard.

"Then why have you led me on for the past two weeks?"

Trent wasn't about to have an argument with a woman who wasn't his woman.

"If that's how you perceived things to be, then I apologize for misleading you," he shrugged, "We can still have fun. I'm just not looking to be in a relationship right now."

"Oh, so now you want me to be like your little hoe?" Natalia was quickly becoming agitated.

Trent shook his head at her choice of wording. He was doing his best to avoid a confrontation with her.

"I wasn't saying that at all. I don't regard you in that manner. I'm confused as to how you thought I was leading you on in any capacity when I made you aware of what was up from the beginning. To keep things from cool between us, what if we just take it slow and figure some things out. Everything doesn't need to be decided right at this moment," he reached for her and placed a kiss on her forehead, "We'll decide on something. Okay?"

Natalia smiled. She loved getting what she wanted and she wanted Trent, so she would have him.

"Okay. That's true. We don't have to make any concrete decisions right at this moment."

"Good." Trent replied going back to his task of tapping his boxes up. "Are you going to need help packing your things?"

"Yo T, you ready?" Trent smiled as his homeboy Kodi popped up at the door interrupting him and Natalia's conversation.

"Yeah. This the last box right here."

"Aight bet." Kodi looked over at Natalia.

"Yo, who is this?"

Trent laughed, "This lil' La La. Remember? From back in the day."

"Stoooop!" Kodi exclaimed, "From around the block? Damn shortie," Kodi looked Natalia up and down, "You're all grown up now huh?"

Natalia cringed at the name La La. Her older brother had given her that name when they were little. She had hoped it would die out over time, but apparently not.

"Aye, yo chill." Trent interjected. He could see Kodi was about to go into full playa mode and even though he and Natalia were friends with benefits trying to figure things out. He wasn't about to let Kodi press up on her. Homeboy or not.

"Oh, my bad. This you T."

"Yea."

"Bet, you got it!"

"Can you two stop acting like I'm not sitting right here? I'm not a piece of meat, you know."

"Sorry baby not trying to make you feel that way." Trent quickly spoke up.

"Oh, so I'm your baby now?" Natalia aimed a soft smile at him.

"Hey, don't get no ideas. Remember what we talked about," he gave her a stern look.

Natalia went up to Trent and gently kissed him.

"No worries, Daddy. I know."

Trent smiled when she said Daddy. That was a new development. He'd never asked her to call him that, but he appreciated it. It was something about being called 'Daddy' that made a man feel like he was king of the palace.

"I'm a go finish packing boo. Have a safe trip back and I'll see you soon." Natalia headed toward the dorm room door blowing kisses on her way out.

Kodi watched as Natalia exited the room. Then, turned to look at Trent, "You tapping that?"

Trent just smiled. "You know I don't talk about that stuff."

"Since when?" Kodi asked shooting Trent a look of surprise. "Shortie bad."

"Yeah, she qualifies."

Kodi laughed when Trent said that.

"T, you crazy as hell." Kodi reached down and began stacking boxes on top of each other,

"How many boxes going down? He squatted down so he could pick up the pile of boxes he'd just stacked.

"The ones in your hand and the ones in the corner. But I'll grab those and that's it."

"Bet. The truck downstairs let's get moving."

"Aight." Trent said as he bent down and picked up his stack of boxes. He was happy to be leaving behind college life.

***

Natalia settled back into the city nicely. Personally, she hated to admit that she enjoyed city life much more than that country living, especially since she'd made such a big deal about moving out there for her friends to get away from the city.

"So explain to me again why you back on this side without receiving your degree?"

Natalia pouted her lips at Erikka's questions.

"Why you all in my business?"

"Ummm because all your stuff moved back in with me before I even saw your face."

Natalia frowned and stared at Erikka not really wanting to discuss anything, but since she was staying with her, she knew she owed her some explanation.

"I don't know E." Natalia sighed. "I don't know what I'm doing. Trent got me bugging. It's as if I have to be around him and in his space, you know? It's crazy."

Erikka watched Natalia in disbelief.

"Nothing is more important than your education. This little obsession you have with Trent is one thing, but don't let that interfere with your schooling. You need to be smart about this."

"I am being smart." Natalia snapped back beginning to take offense. "You act as if I'm not enrolled in school. I'm still on top of my game with that."

Erikka eyed Natalia as if she were delusional.

"I hear what your mouth saying, but let's say Trent up and move to another state or something to get his career up and poppin'. What you gonna do?" Follow him and switch schools again?" Erikka paused, "You need to focus honey because you're not in high school anymore. You're an adult now and you have to act that way. And this behavior you're displaying is pure foolishness."

"Yo E, I am focused." Natalia yelled as she began pacing the floor back forth. "No offense to you, but if I wanted a lecture and an opinion, I would have asked for it." Natalia was now highly irritated and hostile, "Since I did not ask, your unsolicited advice is unwanted. Thanks."

Erikka's brown cat-shaped eyes narrowed when Natalia began to pace and she braced herself for what was coming. She knew how Natalia's temper could be once she felt like she was being attacked in any manner. However, Erikka felt as if she was only trying to help her make good decisions and see to reason. She knew that Natalia wouldn't see it that way and if she hadn't been purely reacting to Natalia's things arriving unexpectedly back at her apartment without notice, she may have approached the topic differently.

"You need to know your place when you speak to me," Natalia continued her rant, "I don't ask you anything about your life and how you're living it. Do I?" Natalia shouted focusing her almond-shaped eyes on Erikka's unmoved face.

"I know my place Na Na." Erikka spoke calmly, not wanting Natalia to flick off because she knew all too well what kind of hellion Natalia was prone to being. In high school, the girl had gotten in more fights than anyone Erikka had ever known. That's why she'd had to be taken out the public school system and had to go to private school. Her temper was like a firecracker always waiting to ignite. "All I'm asking you to do is take some time to think before you act, stop being so impulsive. You and Trent aren't even in a relationship. Does he even care about all the trouble you are going through for him?"

"Shut up Erikka, just shut up! I know what I'm doing!" Natalia yelled, beginning to spazz out.

"Erikka shook her head as Natalia lost her cool Natalia was always such a loose cannon, unable to hold a rational conversation to save her life.

"You need to calm down or you can leave."

"Oh, I'm not leaving and I'm not calming down. Now what?" Natalia threatened, standing erect and ready for anything to pop off.

"Calm down little girl. Think about your actions. You're the one that will end up homeless. I have somewhere to stay." Erikka had tried to play nice, but Natalia's stank attitude was working her nerves. She had no problem going toe-to-toe with Natalia if need be. Her eyes widened suddenly when she saw the crazed look in Natalia's eyes as she went to grab the apple paperweight that Erikka kept on the side table next to the sofa.

Natalia was seeing red. She couldn't really explain what happened in the next second. She only remembered coming to and seeing Erikka laid out on the floor lying in a pool of blood with a gash in her head. Feeling the weight in her hand Natalia glanced down and saw the paperweight that she must have picked up at some point. Dropping the weight on the floor, Natalia bent down to Erikka and held two fingers up to her throat to test for a pulse. She felt a faint pulsing beat under her fingertips.

Natalia continued looking at Erikka feeling no remorse. Looking around the tiny den, Natalia stood and made her way to the sofa and grabbed one of the pillows. Making her way back to Erikka, Natalia shook her head. She'd only needed a place to crash. She had never expected things to escalate to this point. *Why couldn't Erikka just mind her business?* She thought as she bent down and held the pillow over Erikka's face. Slowly beginning to apply pressure Natalia lie on the pillow and shut her eyes.

Waking a short while later to the sound of a singing phone, Natalia couldn't believe that she had fallen asleep. Jumping up to retrieve her phone, Natalia smiled when she saw Trent's name flashing across the screen.

"Hi, Daddy," she said in a sultry voice.

Trent couldn't hold his smile back on the other end of the phone.

"Hey, What you up to?"

Natalia glanced over Erikka's lifeless body lying on the floor and smiled, "Nothing. Just wishing I was with you. What's going on?" She was immune to what had just transpired between her and Erikka. This wasn't the first and probably wouldn't be the last time that someone got in Natalia's way and she had to handle it in her own special manner.

"I want to see you. You all settled in yet? Can I stop by?"

"You know my Daddy can always stop by. What time are you thinking?"

"How about in about thirty minutes?"

"Cool. That's perfect. I'll text you the address."

"Aight bet. See you in a few."

"Kay." Natalia replied hanging up the phone. Moving to the kitchen, Natalia opened the cabinet and pulled out a wine glass, opening the drawer at the counter, she pulled out an automatic corkscrew. Removing a bottle of wine from the refrigerator, she uncorked the wine and poured herself a glass. Taking a long sip, Natalia welcomed the cool liquid flowing through her body. Finishing off the glass, she reached into the cabinet doors under the sink, pulled out latex gloves, bleach, and Pine Sol. Turning on the stereo, Natalia put on her favorite CD and listened to Goldberg Variations by Johann Sebastian Bach in repeat as she cleaned up the mess she'd made by hitting Erikka with a paperweight. Once done, she got a blanket from the guest room and rolled Erikka up inside it. She then dragged her to her room, shut, and locked the door. Natalia rushed to cut on her shower water and gather herself together. She wanted to make sure every hair was in place and she looked like a million bucks when Trent arrived.

***

Trent was about an hour late getting to Natalia's apartment. She lived on the far side of Brooklyn about five stops from Coney Island. He rarely got out on this side, but he'd rather come visit her than let her know where he lived.

Knocking on the door, he waited patiently for Natalia to let him inside.

"Hi Daddy. I've been waiting." Natalia whispered once she opened the door.

31

Moving aside so that Trent could enter, she couldn't wait for the night to begin.

When Trent entered the apartment, he didn't know what to make of the place. It looked as if Natalia had lit every candle known to man. He fully expected the apartment to go up in flames before he left.

"What is that you're listening to?" Trent asked before sitting on the sofa in the living room. "Kind of creepy don't you think?"

Natalia laughed, trying to cover up her horror of leaving the classical music playing. She really didn't want anyone to know about the little things that she did to zone out when she was in her altered frame of mind. Switching the CD off, she quickly switched the music to smooth R&B jams. Aan old Baby Face track began playing.

"I love this song," she smiled as she softly sang the lyrics to whip appeal placing a glass of wine in Trent's hand.

Trent smiled, appreciating her new music choice and her husky singing voice.

"You been missing me?" He asked taking a sip of his wine.

Natalia stopped singing and sat down next to Trent.

"Of course, Daddy. I love you."

Trent almost spat out his wine. He hadn't expected Natalia to use the "L" word.

"Huh?" Trent asked, placing his glass on the table. His eyes seemed as if they wanted to bulge out of his head. Natalia continued taking things so far left where he was concerned. She was creeping him out.

Natalia smiled as she laid her head on his shoulder. "I love you," she repeated.

Trent stood up abruptly, causing Natalia's head to jerk and hit the back of the sofa once his shoulder was suddenly gone from under her head. Suddenly, he felt extremely hot and as though he was suffocating. He needed to get out of Natalia's apartment as soon as possible.

"Where you going?"

Trent cleared his throat. "I just remembered that I've got somewhere that I need to be."

Natalia hopped up off the sofa and grabbed Trent by the arm.

"Wait. Don't leave. You're reading too much into that statement. I just wanted you to know how I felt. Nothing has to change between the two of us."

Trent hesitated before turning back to face Natalia.

"You already know I'm not looking for anything too serious right?" Trent told her in the slow, patient tone. He was tired of having to repeat himself to her, but he needed her to understand. He was used to women having a little crazy in them, but her level of crazy was beginning to shake him. How could she possibly love him already? He knew they had known each other since childhood, but those are kid feelings, as an adult she didn't know too much about her.

"Come on baby," Natalia said pushing him back on the sofa. "We don't have to go into all of that tonight. I already know how you feel about the situation. Let's just relax and enjoy one another's company okay?" Natalia laid half across Trent's lap and began placing light kisses on his neck.

Trent knew he needed to stay away from Natalia, knew that it was probably best to leave her craziness exactly where it needed to be, alone. In spite of herself, he couldn't deny that she was fun and he really enjoyed spending time with her. Feeling himself beginning to falter, he allowed his body to melt under her touch.

The shrill ringing of a cell phone broke up the intimate setting for the two.

Natalia jumped as she tried to figure out where the phone was located. Her heart beating a million miles a minute, she tried to follow the sound of Erikka's phone.

Trent watched as Natalia frantically ran around the tiny apartment, picking up and tossing everything around trying to locate the phone.

"I think it may be in the cushion of that chair over there," he said offering some assistance.

Flashing a grateful smile in his direction, Natalia retrieved the phone and shut it off. She couldn't believe she'd forgotten to turn Erikka's phone off. She was definitely slipping on her game. She never would have done that before, rushing to get ready for Trent had thrown her off her game.

"You okay?" Trent asked noticing how tense she had been over a phone ringing.

"I'm okay. Just forgot to shut that thing off before you came."

"Should I be jealous?" Trent lightly teased.

"Oh please! You never have to be jealous," she exclaimed, "You're all the man I need trust me on that." Natalia slowly licked her lips and winked at him.

Trent smiled as he shook his head. He admired Natalia. She definitely didn't hold back. If she wanted something, she went all in with it.

"Give me one second, I'll be right back."

"Take your time."

Natalia quickly made her way to Erikka's room with the cell phone in tow.

Closing the door softly behind her, she opened the flip phone and saw a missed call from Shay. Redialing Shay's number, she waited patiently for her to answer.

"E what's up, you're late." Shay answered without saying "hello," "That's not like you. Everything okay?"

"Hey Shay. It's Natalia."

"Hey Talli. Where is Erikka?"

Natalia smiled at the nickname that only Shay called her.

"Girl, E drank too much and passed out in her room." Glancing at Erikka's battered, bruised and bloody non-breathing face exposed while the rest of her body was wrapped up in the blanket; Natalia admired her handiwork, "Doesn't look like she'll be going anywhere tonight." *Or ever again,* Natalia thought.

"Really? I'm surprised by that. She was so excited when she called me earlier." Shay paused, "Well okay. Tell E I'll come check on her tomorrow. Later Chick."

"Lata." Natalia hung up the phone.

There, she thought, crisis averted…for now.

Leaving Erikka's body and returning to the living room, Natalia laughed as she saw Trent laid out on the sofa playing with his phone.

Lying directly on top of him interrupting his phone play, Natalia unbuckled his pants, "Okay," she whispered softly gazing up into his eyes, "Where were we?"

Trent let the phone fall to the floor and touched his hands behind his head, "You tell me."

"Shh." Natalia whispered as she pulled his shirt out his pants, "Just enjoy and watch your Mami work."

Trent's lips turned up in a smile as he let her perform her magic. For the rest of the night, the sounds of sexual satisfaction could be heard throughout the apartment.

Chapter 5

It had been a year now and Natalia was happy to be still dating Trent. He had brought her to the Brooklyn Museum and she loved every minute of it.

"Thank you for bringing me here." Trent gazed down at Natalia and smiled, he had to give it to Natalia, she definitely believed in perseverance. She was beginning to make him a believer about maybe entertaining with her.

"You're welcome. I know how much you appreciate art."

Smiling, Natalia nodded her head, "I love it almost as much as I love you."

Trent broke eye contact with Natalia and began looking around the museum.

"Did you hear me?"

Trent sighed, "Yes. I heard you. Can we not get into one of those heavy discussions right now? I brought you here to have a good time, so let's do that okay?" He placed a soft kiss on her forehead and prayed that she would drop the subject.

"You know we've been dating over a year now, right? Shouldn't we discuss what our next step should be?"

"Please babe, not here okay. I promise we will have plenty of time to discuss this okay." Trent raised his eyes to the ceiling. He had been kicking it with Natalia for the last year, to say that they were dating was a stretch, but that wasn't something that he wanted to discuss right now. He didn't want Natalia acting a fool in the museum.

"But when? Whenever, I bring it up you never want to discuss it."

"Please Natalia, I'm asking you as nicely as possible to drop it until later."

"Okay fine. Later will come soon enough."

Trent was upset that she'd taken a perfectly good day and ruined it. Now he was ready to go.

"How about we go look at that piece over there?" Natalia pointed to a far wall in the museum where a colorful display of abstract art was being presented.

"Why don't you go look? I'm a take a breather for a moment."

"Okay. Don't wander off too far." Natalia told him, allowing him a minute to get his breather. She knew she had struck a nerve with wanting to talk about where their *relationship* was headed, but she was determined that he was going to tell her something and he was going to do it today.

If she only knew, Trent thought. He wanted to be as far away from her as possible and to think for a few moments before he had been contemplating actually giving her what she wanted. He was glad he hadn't spoken out on that.

"I won't. Just going to check out some other pieces." Trent walked away without waiting for a response. He wasn't in the mood to deal with Natalia and her dramatic antics today.

Turning the corner, Trent stopped short; there she was. She must have dropped her purse because lip-gloss, pens, makeup, and paper were everywhere. Retrieving her cell, which was next to his foot, Trent approached the amazing looking woman.

"I believe this is yours," he said squatting down next to her.

Glancing up at him, she blushed. Reaching her hand out to grab the phone, she said, "I apologize for it being in the way," she paused as she took all of him in, "I can be such a klutz sometimes."

Gazing into her chocolate almond-shaped eyes, Trent stuck out his hand, "Hi, I'm Trent."

Taking his hand into hers slowly, she said, "Hello, I'm Phylicia," she smiled, "And thanks again for retrieving my phone."

"Not a problem," he replied as he helped her pick up the rest of her things. Lazily standing back to his feet, he reached for her hand to help her rise when they were done.

"I can't thank you enough. What can I do to show my appreciation for your generosity?"

One side of Trent's mouth turned up in a half grin. She had afforded him the perfect opening. Gazing down into her beautiful face, he took in all of her features. She was tall, with an athletic build and a round ass. She reminded him of the actor Salli Richardson.

"You can have dinner with me tonight," he responded.

"Oh, I don't know about that," she said averting her eyes. Trent shrugged pulling out his business card, "Call me if you change your mind," he said handing her his card, then walking away to find Natalia who was standing in the walkway staring at him, watching his exchange with Phylicia through narrowed eyes.

"Who was that?" Natalia asked Trent angrily with fire in her eyes and venom in her voice.

"Yo, don't trip. She dropped her stuff and I helped her pick it up. That's all.

"I saw you hand her your business card." Natalia narrowed her eyes even more staring at Trent through slits. "Why do you need to stay in contact with her if all you were doing was helping her pick her things up off the floor?" Crossing her arms Natalia waited for an appropriate response from him.

"Once again, we are not going to engage in a public display of foolishness. Matter of fact let's go." Trent grabbed her arm and led Natalia toward the door forcefully.

Natalia jerked her arm out of his reach. "Don't manhandle me in that manner," she spoke through clenched teeth. He didn't want a scene, but if he kept at her that's exactly what he was going to get. She was trying to play it cool since she really wanted them to discuss the direction of their relationship.

"Well act like you have some sense and stop embarrassing me all the time."

"I wasn't trying to embarrass you." Natalia whined. Times like this reminded Trent of how young Natalia really was. At nineteen, she wasn't ready for the qualities that he was looking for in a grown woman. Someone like Phylicia he thought; everything about her presentation had impressed him. She'd been dressed in a lavender form fitting dress that hugged all of her curves in the right places. She gave the appearance of being about her business. That's what attracted Trent the most. Glancing down at Natalia, she had a girlish appearance about her and while he found that cute, Phylicia had touched on something deeper than that with him. He wanted to know more about her in every way imaginable.

41

"Well, you may not be trying, but either way you're succeeding." Trent paused before dragging out a long sigh, "Maybe we should take a break from whatever this is we're doing. I need some time to think and see what I'm really doing and if I want you with me or not."

Natalia stopped walking when she heard those words exit Trent's mouth.

"Daddy, whatever I did I'll fix it. I don't want us to take a break. I love you," she began to sob.

Trent flagged down a taxi, mad at himself for not driving on their outing today.

Practically pushing Natalia into the taxi and slamming the door, Trent was ready to be done with the dramatics.

"Please take her wherever she needs to go." Trent told the taxi driver through the window as he handed him a crisp $100 bill.

Trent watched as the taxi sped away with Natalia screaming at him out the window and even though he knew he couldn't get rid of her that easily, he was happy that for this moment, she was gone and he could breathe in his own air again.

***

Trent sat in his office deep in thought. He hoped that Natalia was doing okay. It wasn't like her to go two weeks without speaking to him. He thought that she must really be upset this time. Even though he no longer wanted to deal with her in the capacity that he had been, he still wanted her to be okay.

He smarted a little when his cell began to vibrate on his desk." Trent eyed the number suspiciously, whoever it was wasn't saved in his phone.

"Hello?" Trent cautiously answered his cell phone on the second ring. He was apprehensive about answering numbers he didn't know.

"Hi." A soft milk chocolate voice responded, "This is Phylicia. We met at the Brooklyn Museum."

Phylicia, Trent thought. How could he forget about the woman he met about two weeks ago?

"Phylicia, nice to hear from you. I guess you changed your mind, huh?"

There was a small pause on her end, "I guess so."

"What can I do for you?"

"Well, I was phoning to see if you would be available later this evening."

Trent quickly checked his calendar. He was supposed to go out with Kodi to a new lounge opening in Manhattan, but he was sure Kodi would understand if he cancelled, as much as that dude liked to chase the cat.

"I'm available."

"Wonderful! Text me your address and I'll pick you up around seven."

Trent was shocked that she wanted to pick him up. He couldn't recall a woman ever offering to do that before. He hadn't even had dinner with her yet and her stock value had already increased as far as he was concerned.

"Sounds like a bet. See you at seven," he said hanging up the phone.

Mood instantly lifted, Trent was now having a great afternoon. His desk phone ringing shifted him out of his Phylicia daze.

"Trent speaking." Spoke into the phone receiver.

"Daddy." Natalia whining voice oozed across the line, "Why haven't you called to check for me? I've been missing you."

Trent could have kicked himself for not checking the caller ID before he answered.

"Hey what's up?"

"What's up with you? Where have you been? The way you shoved me into a taxi and kept it moving was unacceptable. You should have called to apologize by now."

"Apologize. For what?" Trent was in shock. He didn't believe for a second that he owed Natalia an apology, but he was anxious to hear why she thought he did.

"For the way you treated me at the museum. What you mean for what? You have some nerve."

"Natalia," Trent said sitting up straight in his chair speaking in a stern tone, "I don't have time for this right now. Instead of a little break, let's just stop dealing with one another, period."

He heard Natalia gasp on the other end of the line.

"You don't mean that," she paused, "I know you don't. You just need a little space right now, so I'll allow you that."

Trent didn't feel like arguing with her. "Fine, whatever. I'm hanging up now." Without waiting for a response, Trent placed the phone back in its cradle.

Glancing at the clock, it read 5:45 PM. Trent stood and grabbed his suit jacket from the back of his chair. Natalia had almost ruined his mood, but thinking of how sweet that it would be to see Phylicia tonight lifted his spirits immensely.

***

Phylicia parked her all-black Benz in front of the address Trent had texted her and pulled out her cell.

"I'm outside," she said after she dialed his number and he answered.

Waiting patiently for him to come down, Phylicia pulled the car visor down and looked at her face in the mirror. Seeing faint traces of puffiness under her left eye, she pushed the visor back up disgusted. Leaning her head back on the headrest, she closed her eyes and prayed for peace.

Suddenly opening her eyes when a knock came at her window, Phylicia smiled at how handsome Trent looked while holding an all-white bouquet of roses with a solitaire royal blue one in the middle. Pressing the button to unlock the door, she watched as Trent slid into the car with ease.

"You really didn't have to bring these roses, though they are very beautiful," she beamed a smile at him.

"Beautiful roses for beautiful woman." Trent replied as he shut the car door. Leaning in slightly he placed a soft gentle kiss on Phylicia's cheek.

Phylicia welcomed his sweet kiss on her cheek.

"Thank you for coming out with me tonight. I just want to get out and have a nice time." Phylicia stated as she pulled the Benz away from the curb.

"That's something that I think I can handle." Trent replied.

Phylicia turned her head slightly his way and looked at him out the corner of her eye. "Show you a nice time, I mean." Trent stammered.

Phylicia muffled a laugh. "Relax. You're doing a great job already," she told him.

"So, where are we going? Better yet, where are you kidnapping me to?"

Phylicia flashed perfect teeth at him, "You'll see. It's a surprise," she paused, "And I'm not kidnapping you...yet."

***

Just as I suspected. Natalia thought as she had the taxi driver follow the Benz at a slow pace. She knew there had to be another woman in the mix because Trent had literally gone M.I.A. on her for the past few weeks and that wasn't like him at all. Break or no break.

"Miss." The cab driver began in an impatient tone, "Is there somewhere I can drop you?"

46

"I am paying you three hundred dollars for your time. You are going to follow that black car with no further commentary understand?" She asked in a tone filled with malice.

The cab driver eyed her through the rearview mirror with a smirk on his face, gazing at the petite woman with amusement dancing in his eyes. Even though she was dressed in all-black with a NY cap pulled down over her face, he was not feeling threatened in the least little bit.

Natalia saw the amusement on the driver's face and before he knew what hit him, she had a switchblade to the back of his neck.

"Now, I don't see anything funny. Do you?" The driver shook his head.

"Good. Now continue driving and not another word."

They drove on in silence as Natalia pulled out her cell phone and dialed Trent's number.

Trent felt his phone vibrating at his hip. When he glanced down and saw Natalia's name flashing on the screen he quickly hit ignore.

Natalia was furious when she heard Trent's voicemail pick up "I know he didn't just send me to voicemail," she mumbled.

Dialing his number, again Natalia waited impatiently and in vain for him to pick up his phone. When he sent her to voicemail again, she nearly blew a gasket.

"Please pull over in that alley and let me out," she addressed the taxi driver.

Immediately switching lanes and jerking the taxi to a stop at the curb, the driver waited.

Natalia put her phone back in her purse and focused on the driver.

"Thank you so much for your cooperation. You've been most helpful," she commented before shoving the switchblade into the back of the driver's neck and watched as his eyes widened in shock at what was happening to him. Before he could yell out, Natalia jerked the knife up and twisted it until his gurgling noises ended. Removing the knife from his neck, she wiped it clean on his shirt. She then collected her three hundred dollars back from him off the front seat where he had sat it, then exited the taxi as if nothing had ever happened, walking away down the street and around the corner as if she were on nothing more than an evening stroll.

***

Phylicia had taken Trent to Eleven Madison Park, which was a high end restaurant located in lower Manhattan on 11 Madison Ave and Gramercy & Flatiron. Trent had never been to this particular restaurant before and was elated to be trying something new.

"This is nice," he said once the Maître D had seated them and he took in the balcony-level private dining room that they were in that overlooked the main dining room and offered a view of Madison Square Park through 20-foot windows.

"Yeah, this is one of my favorite places to come to."

"And you brought me here? What, am I special or something?" Trent smiled at her.

Phylicia gave him a sad smile, "Not yet, but maybe one day."

Trent laughed, "There's a lot to be said for someone being brutally honest huh?"

"Sorry." Phylicia instantly apologized. "I wasn't trying to offend."

"No offense taken over here."

"Good. I hate when a man is extremely sensitive. That's an immediate turn off for me."

"I can understand that." Trent replied. "Why is this your favorite place to come to?" He asked, attempting to change the subject.

"Yes please." Phylicia said when a waiter came by with a bottle of wine to fill their wine glasses and left the bottle chilling on the table. Once the waiter was done, Phylicia thanked him and then refocused her attention on Trent.

"I like coming here because only a certain level of clientele can get in. Reservations need to be made in advance and the head cost per plate is roughly a little shy of two hundred dollars," she said gazing over at Trent. That usually cuts down on the riff raff. My life is colorful enough, so I love the serenity this place offers me."

Trent almost choked on his glass of wine when she said prices ran towards two hundred a plate. Not that he couldn't afford it, but he had never spent that much on the first date with any woman. He was flattered by the fact that Phylicia thought enough of him to spend that amount of money.

"Why is your life so colorful?"

Phylicia shook her head. "I just always have so much going on. Being a lawyer, I see unique actions every day, most of which come from the clients that I deal with day in and out and some family issues that I have."

"Do you want to talk about this?" Trent asked sensing that this wasn't a topic that she favored.

"Not really," she responded flashing a grateful smile in his direction.

"Ok, I'm going to run to the restroom and come back."

"Okay. I'll be here." Phylicia replied holding up her glass as if she were about to give a toast.

When Trent came back to the table, Phylicia had ordered them another bottle of wine.

"Rough day?" Trent laughed.

"Rough life." Phylicia responded.

Trent sat down as the waiter began serving them the first course of their meal. "Rough life huh? That's deep. Do you want to talk about it?"

Phylicia shook her head no and kept drinking. By the third course, Phylicia had been on to yet another bottle of wine after consuming the prior one almost entirely alone.

"You've been good company tonight. Thank you for allowing me to forget for just a little while. I needed to laugh and you gave me that. I really appreciate you."

"Glad I could be of service to you." Trent told her.

Putting down her glass she raised her hands to hold her head and turned to face him, "I think I've had a little too much to drink," she whispered.

"That's alright." Trent said not in the least bit surprised considering all the alcohol that she had consumed that evening, as he stood and helped her to her feet. "We can go. I promise to take good care of you."

"Aren't you sweet?" Her words slurred as she leaned heavily onto Trent, "Oh wait," she stopped short, "I have to pay."

"Don't worry. I already covered the bill long before now. Let's go." Trent gently placed a hand under her elbow and guided her to the exit of the restaurant.

"Oh, that's so nice." Phylicia spoke in her slurred speech.

"Where is the valet ticket?" Trent asked her, trying to get answers before she fell asleep. "In your purse?"

"Mmhmmn." Phylicia mumbled. Trent could see that she was quickly fading.

Handing the ticket to the valet Trent waited outside with Phylicia leaning on his side. Once the Benz pulled up, Trent paid the valet and tipped him handsomely.

Trent opened the passenger door and deposited Phylicia safely inside. Moving to the driver's side, he got behind the wheel and pulled off.

Seeing that Phylicia was in no condition to chat because she hadn't been in the car for two minutes and was already fast asleep, Trent made the decision to take her to his place because he didn't know where she lived.

Pulling up to his condo, Trent was lucky to find a parking space out in front. That was something that usually never happened. Parallel parking the Benz, Trent hopped out, opened Phylicia's door, and smiled. She was completely knocked out. Bending down into the car, he gently scooped her up into his arms and closed the doors locking them with the key pad.

Natalia stood across the street watching from the shadows as Trent cradled the woman in his arms. *He's taking that wreck up to his place.* She thought as she watched him disappear into his building. She had been smart to wait for them here. She'd known that Trent would bring her back to his place, which had Natalia's blood boiling because he had never allowed her in his place. She'd had to follow him one evening to figure out where he lived.

Dashing across the street as the doors closed behind them, Natalia waited a few minutes before entering. Taking the stairs two at a time to the fifth floor where Trent lived, Natalia exited the stairwell and proceeded to his door. Pressing her ear to the door, Natalia listened to see if she could make out any sounds coming from the other side. Hearing nothing but silence in return, Natalia backed away from the door trying to think of a way to get inside of the condo. She knew that the building he lived in had floor-to-ceiling windows in the different condo's bedroom. She'd had pretended to be in the market to buy and had a realtor bring her out to see one so that she could get a feel for the layout in the event that she ever needed to; something like she was about to do now. Knowing about the windows however didn't help her because she knew there was nothing on the outside of them for her to stand on.

Natalia stood there for a moment, thinking and then her eyes lit up like the fourth of July when it dawned on her that there was a ledge underneath the bathroom window. Moving swiftly toward the window down at the end of the long hallway, Natalia pushed it open and stepped onto the ledge. Being careful to not lose her balance, she slowly walked to the ledge until she arrived to the spot below Trent's bathroom window and waited.

Trent laid Phylicia down in his bed, went to his armoire, and pulled out one of his t-shirts. Going back to the bed, he gradually sat Phylicia up and unzipped her dress. Averting his eyes from her body out of respect, he smoothly pulled the t-shirt onto her body. Removing her shoes, he laid her back down and pulled the comforter up to her chin. Placing a soft kiss on her forehead, he stepped away from her to lay her dress over the black leather recliner that he had in the corner of his bedroom. Exiting the room, Trent retired to the living room. Removing his shirt and slacks, he got comfortable in his boxers with no shirt. Picking up the remote from his glass coffee table he was about to cut the TV on when he thought he heard a noise coming from the bathroom.

Quietly setting the remote down, Trent went to his safety box under the TV and pulled out his gun. Ever since Kodi had gone into law enforcement, he had insisted that Trent become licensed to have a weapon too. Kodi stood by this quote for all time, "if all the criminals have weapons, then the non-criminals needed them as well, to keep an order of balance," he'd say.

Grateful now for following his advice, Trent silently made his way toward the bathroom door and waited.

Natalia was doing her best to not make a lot of noise. Now that she was inside, she was going to see first hand what Trent and his little date were up too.

Listening for any sound of movement, Natalia moved cautiously to open the door when she heard nothing.

Seeing the door creep open Trent cocked the gun back and got ready to pull the trigger. Natalia saw a shadow out the corner of her eye and immediately dropped to the floor.

"Don't!" She yelled.

Trent stopped when he heard the familiar female voice.

"Natalia?" He asked, uncocking the gun and cutting the light on, "What are you doing?"

Natalia knew that she was cold busted.

"I was worried that something had happened to you. You didn't answer my calls, so I thought you may have been in here unconscious or something," she said, thinking of a lie on the fly, while brushing herself off as she got up off the floor.

Putting the gun on the table Trent eyed Natalia as if she were crazy.

"Seriously?" You really thought that I was in here unconscious because I didn't answer your calls?" Trent wasn't buying her story even a little bit.

"I did Daddy." Natalia's eyes took a quick sweep of the room before she pressed her body up against Trent's since she didn't notice anything out of the ordinary. Presently not caring what happened to the woman who Trent had carried inside.

Trent gently, but firmly moved her away from him.

"You need to leave," he told her.

"Leave?" Natalia gave him a look of disbelief. "I just got here."

"Firstly, you broke in. I don't care what kind of crazy excuse you use as a means for doing it." Trent told her shooting her a pointed look. "Second. I have company and I don't want them disturbed."

Taking notice of Trent's state of undress for the first time, Natalia was angry.

"I bet you don't want to be disturbed. We've only been on a break for two weeks, I saw you carry that woman inside, and what do you think you're doing?" Her voice steadily escalating.

Grabbing her arm hard Trent pulled her toward the door. "We were never in a relationship. This is exactly what I need a break from. You're doing too much and need you to leave."

Natalia looked down at his hand holding her arm in a vise grip and narrowed her eyes.

"I'm not going anywhere?" She spoke in a low tone.

"I hope you don't call yourself, telling me what you're going to be doing in my own place."

Natalia stood her ground. "I'm not leaving as long as that woman is here."

Trent didn't argue with Natalia, he tightened his grip on her arm and continued pulling her toward the door. Opening the door, he pulled her out into the hallway.

"Please don't embarrass yourself further. Go home and don't try to come through my bathroom window again because it will be bolted and I am having an alarm system put in place in the morning."

"You really don't have to act like that." Trent closed the door in her face. She really was a crazy hoe. It wasn't that he was trying to be rude, but Natalia needed to learn her place and there was no time like the present for that to happen.

Chapter 6

Phylicia woke the next day with a massive headache. Turning her head slowly not to increase the pain, she was feeling she realized she had no idea where she was. Forcing her brain to work, she tried to recall the details of her evening.

She remembered picking up Trent and going to the restaurant for dinner and that's when the memories stopped. Lifting the comforter, so that she could stand up, Phylicia realized that she was in a t-shirt. Quickly glancing around the room, she noticed her clothes lying on the chair in the corner.

This has to be Trent's place. She thought, trying to keep herself from going ballistic. That's the only thing that was logical to her because she knew Trent wouldn't just leave her out to dry. Standing slowly, she managed to walk to the bedroom door and open it without falling flat on her face.

Trent glanced up when Phylicia came out of the bedroom looking completely disoriented, but still very sexy to him.

"Nice to have you up and alert." Trent smiled at her, "Good morning."

"Morning." Phylicia responded in a groggy voice barely recognizable to her own ears. Moving slowly toward Trent, she sat at the edge of the sofa. "What happened last night?" She asked pushing her unruly hair out of her eyes.

"Before, during or after you passed out in the car. I brought you here, undressed you; my favorite part," He winked at her, "Put you in my t-shirt, and tucked you in bed for the night. I slept out here on the sofa."

"Oh," she said softly, "I'm sorry to impose on you like this. I'm usually pretty good about holding my liquor." Phylicia looked at him sheepishly.

"You're not imposing at all. I enjoyed your company before you passed out," he joked, winking at her.

Phylicia rested her head on the back of the sofa and closed her eyes. "I'll leave as soon as I get my clothes on."

"Take your time, no rush. Are you hungry?" When Phylicia didn't respond to his question, Trent looked at her and noticed that she had fallen back to sleep.

Retrieving the comforter from the back room, Trent moved Phylicia's body so that she was lying flat on the sofa and put the blanket on top of her.

Gazing down at her, he marveled at how beautiful she was. He couldn't wait for the opportunity to touch her the way that he really wanted.

Seeking out the Advil in the medicine cabinet of the bathroom, he went into the kitchen and removed a bottle of water from his refrigerator and put both on the coffee table in front of the sofa so that the next time Phylicia was awake she would see it and take it. He knew that her head had to be killing her.

Phylicia woke a couple of hours later to the smell of something cooking. The aroma had her mouth watering. Sitting up she saw the Advil and bottled water that Trent had left for her on the coffee table and smiled, as she took the pills and drank some water. He was so attentive she thought; she really liked that quality about him.

Paddling barefoot into the kitchen still clad in Trent's t-shirt that barely came down to the middle of her thighs; Phylicia stood in the doorframe and observed him move around with ease. Drinking more water from the bottle, she sat on the floor Indian-style and continued watching him in silence.

Trent was oblivious to the fact that Phylicia had arisen and that he was now providing her with live entertainment. Setting the plates on the table, he was jammin' to the Nas hit, Ether. He made him and Phylicia smothered turkey wings, steamed rice, baked sweet potatoes, buttered asparagus, and rolls for dinner. Phylicia had practically slept the day away and he knew that she would be hungry when she finally did get up from her nap.

"Smells pretty amazing." Phylicia said from the floor alerting him to the fact that she was awake and watching him.

Trent turned to face her and marveled at how adorable she looked sitting on the floor Indian-style with her hair all over her head. He liked that she didn't trip off her appearance as so many other women do.

"How long have you been sitting there?"

"Not too long."

"Can I join you?" Trent asked her already removing the plates from the table.

"Sure." Phylicia responded amused when he transferred everything from the table to the floor. "This is a first for me. I've never had dinner quite like this before."

"Glad to be breaking new ground with you." Trent finished placing everything on the floor for them. "How is your head feeling?"

"Better." Phylicia said pushing her hair to the side, "Guess I needed one more round of sleep, so that I could function."

"And now you need food, so eat." Trent commanded.

"Yes Sir," she laughed as she grabbed the fork off the plate Trent had made for her. Placing some of the turkey wing in her mouth Phylicia closed her eyes as it melted on her tongue. "Oh my goodness, this is good. You outdid yourself. I didn't know you could cook. You neglected to mention that at dinner."

"Just a little something I threw together for you." Trent shrugged. "No biggie."

"You do a good job throwing something together."

"Thank you, thank you." Trent replied as they enjoyed their second evening together.

***

"Yo T, where you been?"

"G-macking."

"What you know about G-macking? Cut it out. What's good with you?"

"I think I'm about to hang it up T and turn in my card."

"Stoooooop playing. You serious?" Kodi said in disbelief, "With La La?"

"Nah, this new shortie I met a couple of weeks ago."

"You only known her a couple of weeks and you already ready to hang it up? You sure about that?"

"K, it's a wrap. She had your boy in here cooking a couple of weeks ago."

"You lyyyying." Kodi laughed on the other end of the line, "What were you cooking?"

"Turkey wings with gravy, rice, sweet potatoes, and asparagus."

"Stoooooop!" Kodi shouted with laughter, "She got you whipped like that son? Her pussy must be fire."

"I wouldn't know." Trent's matter of fact statement brought Kodi's hysterical laughter to a halt.

"Wait, you telling me she got you this whipped, and you ain't even hit yet?" Kodi's voice no longer held traces of laughter. His tone was serious. "Damn."

"I'm telling you, she's perfect. You gotta meet her. You and Sherri should stop by and chill when y'all free."

"Aight bet. Let's do it tomorrow." I gotta meet her and see what got you bugging like this."

"I ain't buggin'. Just met her at the right time I guess."

"Right time my ass."

"Aight. Holla at me tomorrow." Trent laughed at Kodi's sarcasm.

***

Phylicia was cool with hanging out with Trent's friends for the evening. She loved the energy and excitement that he brought to her life.

Kissing her lightly on the cheek once she arrived at his condo Trent loved the way Phylicia looked. Her long hair hung loosely down her back as if he loved it. She had on black leggings and a loose-fitting sky-blue top that hung off her shoulders and matching flats.

Phylicia was beginning to think of Trent as her man. She knew with her circumstances being what they were that she shouldn't think that way, but she was definitely feeling him and not just no little bit. He was sexy to her, much sexier than to what she was accustomed. She was used to only looking at men's physical attributes when thinking of getting with them, but Trent was sexy on so many levels, mind, body, everything. Standing at an even six feet tall, with curly black hair and an athletic build, she could imagine kissing every inch of him until he begged her to stop.

"Thank you for coming tonight to meet my friends."

"There's nowhere that I would rather be than right here with you," she smiled up at him.

"I appreciate that." Trent returned her smile gazing into her brown eyes. "They should be here soon, so make yourself comfortable."

"Thanks, I will."

By the time Kodi and Sherri arrived, Trent made sure that Phylicia had a drink in her hand and he'd pre-poured glasses for Kodi and Sherri as well.

"Ok, time for introductions." Trent began, "Phylicia, this is my man Kodi and his woman Sherri. K and I have kicked it since we were kids."

Phylicia smiled at them both as she shook their hands. "It is such a pleasure to meet you two."

Sherri smiled, "It's nice to see Trent settling down." You're the first woman he's ever introduced."

"Really?" Phylicia began cheesing when Sherri made her statement and turned to face Trent, "So you're settling down are you?" she raised glowing eyes to meet his amused ones.

Trent smiled down at her, "Something like that, if she's interested."

"Definitely interested," she said as she began to melt underneath his gaze.

Trent had to restrain himself from kissing her and stroking her long and hard in front of Kodi and Sherri. The sexual frustration between him and Phylicia was getting out of hand. He had spent the last few weeks allowing her space and not wanting to press her to do anything, so each time they had seen each other, he had never made any sexual advances toward her. They still hadn't been intimate with each other and the anticipation was beginning to kill him slowly every time that he saw her.

Sherri could see the sexual tension between the two herself and was amused by it. She never had a chance to see Trent in this type of situation, so it was definitely entertaining.

"So Phylicia, what do you do?" Sherri asked as she took a seat on the sofa, where treat had set up a couple of veggie snacks, water, so they could just sit, and chill, getting to know one another.

"I'm a Lawyer."

"Word?" Sherri perked up instantly, "Can I get your card? I'm always in need of a good Lawyer."

Phylicia retrieved her purse from the sofa in the living room and pulled out one of her business cards to give to Sherri.

"Why are you always in need of a good Lawyer?" Phylicia was curious.

"Because she can't keep her temper in check." Kodi interjected.

Trent laughed, "Yeah. Sherri can be somewhat of a firecracker."

"Whatever Trent," Sherri laughed throwing a crumbled up napkin at him.

"You get that rowdy?" Phylicia asked her curiously.

"Girl, you just never know! These women out here be getting out of hand," Sherri held up Phylicia's business card, "Trust me girl, dealing with this one over here," she pointed at Kodi, "I'm definitely going to need you."

"Call me any time." Phylicia laughed at Kodi's shocked face and Sherri's bluntness. She was happy to have met Trent's friends. They were quite a pair. As the evening grew later, Phylicia couldn't think of another time she had such a great adult evening of just chatting and shooting the breeze.

"Aight T, me and Sherri bout to head out."

"Bet. Thanks for coming."

"Anytime. It was nice meeting you Phylicia," Sherri smiled and held up the business card Phylicia had given her, "I'll be in touch girl."

"Ok. Nice meeting you two as well." Phylicia smiled, yelling after them as they made their way out the door.

"Your friends are very interesting. I like them." Phylicia stated as she began cleaning up their dirty dishes.

"Yeah, they're cool." Trent said coming up behind Phylicia and removing the dishes out of her hand. Kissing the back of her neck Trent couldn't wait another second. He had to taste her. Picking her up and placing her on the counter Trent stood in between her legs and kissed her gently on the lips, their breaths mingling in sync.

"I want you." Trent whispered into her parted lips.

"I want you too." Phylicia responded breathlessly as she ran her fingers up Trent's long well defined muscular arms.

Trent's hand moved to Phylicia's waist as he sought out the waistband to her leggings. Running his fingers in between her skin and the material, he gently pulled her leggings down to her ankles and stopped. Bending down, he removed her blue flats all her feet and then took her soft pedicured foot in his hand and began to massage each of her toes individually. Phylicia leaned back arching her spine and closed her eyes enjoying the sensation of Trent massaging each of her toes. When the sensation changed as she felt the flick of his tongue at the arch of her foot Phylicia was afraid, she would turn into a water puddle right there on the countertop.

"Oh yes." Phylicia mumbled softly.

Trent loved the response that he was getting from her. Reaching his hands up pulled her leggings the rest of the way down off her foot. Trent was focused on one thing and one thing only; he needed to see how Phylicia tasted. He had fantasized about this moment since he met her.

"You smell so good." Trent whispered huskily as he kissed that inside her ankles before trailing his kisses further up her leg.

Phylicia's sensory glands opened up. It had been so long since she'd been intimate with anyone. Everything Trent was doing to her was setting her soul on fire. As Trent trailed moist kisses up her thigh, Phylicia knew that she was seconds away from losing it.

"Slow down Mami, wait for me." Trent whispered in between kisses. He could sense Phylicia's excitement, but didn't want the night to end prematurely for either of them. Trent stopped kissing the inside of her thigh and began massaging it instead.

Phylicia lifted her eyelids as far as she could get them to go, which was barely a slit and began to calm down.

Trent heard Phylicia's breathing go back to normal and kept massaging her thighs.

"That feels nice." Phylicia murmured.

"You haven't felt nice yet. Just relax and let me work my magic on you."

Phylicia smiled and laid flat against the counter allowing the magician to work.

***

Natalia watched Trent make love to Phylicia on the counter from her view in the darkened hallway. She had just climbed through the bathroom window and crept into this scenario. Hot moisture trailing down her face, she watched as he pulled her panties down and let his tongue run lapse at the apex of her thighs. Natalia could see the passion and fierceness in Phylicia's face as she climaxed. Reminiscing about how Trent used to do the same thing to her, Natalia pulled out a small video camera and silently videoed Trent entering Phylicia's secret treasure and captured the look or pure ecstasy displayed on both of their faces.

***

Phylicia moaned loudly as she and Trent climaxed in unison. "Oh my God, you are amazing," she gasped trying to regulate her breathing and get it back to a normal pattern, "Can we please do that again?"

"If not, why not?" Trent replied seductively with a smile on his face. This was the first time his emotions had been stamped all over a first sexual encounter with a woman. He was glad he and Phylicia had waited and got to know each other a little better.

Phylicia leaned her head to the side and laughed, "You're silly."

"Come on." Trent said lifting her off the countertop and into his arms, carrying her to his bedroom.

"What do you say, up for a round two?" He whispered into her hair.

Phylicia gazed into Trent's eyes and her heart swelled at what she saw displayed there.

"Definitely up for round two," she laughed, kissing him on the nose before he gently placed her on the bed and began kissing her neck signaling that round two was now in full swing.

***

Natalia had barely climbed back out the bathroom window before Trent and Phylicia had headed for the bedroom. Trent had never made good on his promise to get the bathroom window bolted or an alarm installed. Natalia smiled. By the time she completed what she had in mind, he was going to wish that he had.

***

Trent woke the next morning to the smell of turkey sausage sizzling and the aroma of blueberries. Retrieving his boxers off the floor, Trent quickly put them on and followed the smells in the kitchen.

"Good morning honey."

Trent's spirits; though already high; rose even more at the sight of Phylicia in the kitchen prancing around with no clothes on, with her unruly hair cascading wildly down her back.

"Honey is exactly the word I would use to describe how you taste," he said as he approached her and enveloped her in his arms; tonguing her down. "Good morning," he said.

"Wow. It definitely is now." Phylicia huffed trying to catch her breath, "Yes it is a good morning."

Trent sat down at the table as Phylicia brought him a glass of orange juice. Distracted by her nude ass walking by, Trent missed the comment she'd just made.

"Sorry, what did you say?"

Phylicia laughed, "If you focus more on what I'm saying and less on my body maybe you could hear me and we could have a conversation," she scolded lightly.

"My focus is exactly where it needs to be," Trent said reaching out and smacking her ass as she walked by to get the blueberry muffins off the counter. Phylicia laughed and swatted at his hand. After placing the muffins on the table, she went to retrieve her cell phone from her purse.

"I can't keep getting caught up in this fairytale with you." Noticing that she had twenty-seven missed calls, she arched her brow, "My clients need me."

Trent stuffed a muffin in his mouth and shrugged, cheesing like a schoolboy.

Checking her voicemail, Phylicia needed to see what was so urgent.

"Oh my gosh, Phylicia! You need to check your work email sent messages. Where are you? Your naked ass is plastered all over the office network. Call me back right now!" Phylicia's heart began racing as she listened to message after message from her friends and co-workers saying she was blasted all over the internet. Snapping her phone shut, she was angry.

"Do you have a computer?"

Trent's jerked his attention away from his food and in her direction at her tone.

"Yeah, my laptop is over there by my briefcase. Why? What's wrong?" His voice low and concerned.

"We are about to see." Pulling out Trent's laptop, Phylicia logged into her email to see to what everyone was referring. Going into her sent messages, she saw one titled *Countertop Loving*, which had been sent at three thirty that morning. Opening the email, Phylicia braced herself and then her face registered shock and disgust. She was appalled by what she was seeing.

"How could you do this?" She screamed.

"Do what?" Trent jumped up from the table, "Why are you so upset?"

"This!" Phylicia literally threw the laptop at him.

Trent caught his laptop before it crashed to the ground and turned the screen to face him. His eyes widened as he viewed himself driving in and out of Phylicia's wetness on his countertop.

Looking up at her, he watched her angrily throw her clothes on.

"I trusted you!"

"Yo P, I didn't do this."

71

"Yeah." Phylicia screamed, "Well who did? Huh! How could you do this? That email went out to all my colleagues and friends. I could lose my job over this, you, you BASTARD!" She spat.

Pulling Phylicia into his arms, even though she fought him, he refused to let her go.

"Listen to me, just listen. Calm down." However, Phylicia couldn't calm down. She was royally pissed off.

"GET OFF ME!" Phylicia yelled, trying her best to get away from him.

"Not until you listen." Trent yelled back at her.

"Fine. Talk." Phylicia finally said since there was no way that she could overpower him.

"I think I may know what happened."

"I'm listening." Phylicia wanted to do him bodily harm, but he had her whole body pinned against him.

"There's this woman I was previously dating; she may have done it because she's broken into my place before. The first night you stayed over to be exact."

"What? You got some psycho ex-girlfriend that breaks in and out of your house and you think that's okay?" Phylicia was still irritated, "Do you not know anything? That is considered breaking and entering. You should have had her arrested!"

"I thought I had handled it."

"Well it's obvious that you did not!" Phylicia was still angry, but not so much at Trent as she was this random person. Having calmed down a little, she really didn't feel that it was in Trent's character to have them engaging in sex on the internet, from what she knew about him so far. "And somehow, she got access to my email and sent out that total invasion of privacy." Phylicia was disgusted. "Who is this skank? I will be suing her first thing in the morning."

"She's just a kid."

"A kid about to be sued." Phylicia wasn't having it, "Kid or no kid; this is inappropriate behavior, and she needs to be taught a lesson."

"Please let it go." Trent requested of her slowly. He knew that Natalia had to be the one responsible for this, but he wouldn't tell Phylicia that tidbit of information.

"So you know who did this and you aren't going to tell me?" Phylicia said slowly in disbelief.

"I want you to deal with it internally at the office end and then let it go." Trent told her.

Phylicia stared at Trent a long time before she accepted what it was. It's not as if she could take back her assets being displayed for the world to see. Phylicia shook her head.

"Her little ass should be sued." Phylicia snapped. She couldn't understand how Trent could be so nonchalant about this whole matter. Her whole ass was on display for everyone to see. "Matter of fact, how old is she?"

"Nineteen." Trent smiled a sexy grin at her. "See, so you don't really want to sue her. She's just a kid with no direction. Let me handle it."

"Ok fine, handle it. You're lucky I like you because trust me; this would end up completely different if I went about it my way. I'm not into this entire little schoolgirl games. I have a real career and I'm not to be played with."

Trent finally let Phylicia go and smiled down at her. "I knew that you would see it my way. What are you going to tell your job?"

"The truth. That someone hacked my account and invaded our privacy. We'll see what happens." Grabbing her purse, she kissed Trent and headed for the door. "I have to go and do damage control. Give me a call later to make sure I haven't decided to go ahead with my initial course of action and sue this random girl," she said as she headed off to work shutting Trent's apartment door behind her.

***

"Are you really this crazy?" Natalia moved her cell phone away from her ear, so that Trent's booming voice didn't burst her eardrum. It was ringing as it was from the octave of his voice.

"I'm not sure I know what you mean?" Natalia responded calmly into the phone playing dumb as if she didn't know what Trent was referencing.

"You know exactly what I mean. Where are you?" Trent wasn't in the mood for Natalia's antics today.

74

"I'm at home silly. Where else would I be?" Natalia asked sweetly into the phone.

"Good." Trent responded. Natalia glanced up when a knock came at her door, "Open the door," he said.

Natalia hung up the phone and went to the door glancing through the peephole. Sure enough, Trent was on the other side of her door. Slowly undoing the three bolts on the door Natalia jumped back when Trent flung the door open and slammed it shut behind him. She had never seen him this angry before.

Not bothering to mask his anger, Trent began shouting immediately. "You leaked those photos of Phylicia and I, didn't you? Don't even embarrass yourself; I know that you did it."

"Wait, let me explain."

"There is nothing for you to explain. Anything that you and I had going is over and done. Do you understand? You crossed the line this time." Trent was so angry with Natalia that he wanted to do physical harm to her and he had never been one to want to put his hands on a woman, but Natalia was pushing him to the edge.

"I don't know what you're talking abo--"

"YES YOU DO!" Trent said punching his fist into the wall as he cut her off. "Stop playing games. This is the reason you can't be my woman. This right here. You play too many games. I don't have time for it any longer."

"Daddy, I love you."

"I don't care. Stay away from me and any company that I have in my home. Stay away from my home or you leave me no choice but to pursue legal action. Do you understand me?" Trent glared into Natalia's eyes.

"I understand you, but that doesn't mean I have to listen to it." Natalia stated.

"You've been warned. Stay away from me. I want nothing to do with you." Trent left Natalia's house, he could no longer deal with the little childish games. After meeting Phylicia, he only wanted a grown woman and Natalia had a lot of growing to do, she wasn't the one for him.

***

"So you say that you've handled the situation?" Phylicia asked Trent when they were in bed that night. She loved the feeling she got when they laid in bed together and cuddled.

"Yes, it's been handled."

"Good. Because I would hate to have to have your little *girlfriend* locked up." Phylicia said mocking the unknown girl who had breached her privacy, "By the way, I absolutely love the new alarm system."

Trent let out a low laugh that Phylicia felt under her cheek as she laughed on his chest. "I figured you would like that," he leaned his head down and tipped Phylicia's head up, so he could gaze into her eyes, "And the only girlfriend I have running around here is you. You got it?" He asked placing a gentle kiss on her lips.

"Definitely got it," she whispered on his lips.

Loath to break their kiss Trent did so anyway, "How did your job react to the news?"

Phylicia shook her head. "I was so embarrassed when I went into the office. Everyone was looking at me and whispering. My supervisor called me into his office as soon as he saw me. Luckily, they know me pretty well. I've been with my firm since I interned during my law school days, so they knew something crazy must have happened. I just explained that my email had been hacked by this guy that I was dating's crazy ex-girlfriend and he told me he understood, but to not let my private life interfere with my work again. I got the hint. Told him it was a one time thing and that I had everything under control."

"I'm glad that everything worked itself out." Trent said, his lips capturing hers into an intensely sexually charged kiss. Phylicia welcomed his kiss and deepened it as she made love to her man for the majority of the night.

Chapter 7

Phylicia was floating on cloud nine. For the past year and a half, things with her and Trent had progressed nicely and she was in heaven. Trent had invited her to move in with him almost a year prior and she had graciously accepted. She was now happily expecting and due any day now. Not that this whole situation wasn't without incident because she'd had her own demons to deal with, but she'd never let Trent know about it. She would take it to her grave.

"I'm home." Phylicia announced walking through the door to find Trent sitting on the sofa that was facing the door, staring at her with hurt and hatred in his eyes.

"You're married?" He asked solemnly, with his emotions displayed upon his face.

Phylicia felt as someone had sucked the life out of her. The color drained from her face and she began to panic.

"Don't even bother trying to deny it. I have a copy of your marriage certificate right here."

"How did you get that?" Phylicia managed to push the words past her lips.

"Doesn't matter. I can tell by your face that it's true."

"Baby wait." Phylicia cried, "It's not what you think."

"Or," Trent stood up, "It's exactly what I think."

"Just hear me out."

"There's nothing to hear out. I want you to leave." If she hadn't been pregnant, Trent would have been tempted to do bodily harm to her. Then, a thought dawned on him.

"Is the baby even mine?"

Phylicia swallowed hard, "Of course it is," she began shaking, and then looked down in disbelief as moisture began to seep down her legs. Her water broke.

"We'll see about that." Trent was angry and hurt. He wanted to throw Phylicia into a wall for making him feel this way. What were with the women whom he had chosen lately? They made him want to inflict pain on him when he just wanted to be the nice guy.

"Trent." Phylicia's voice was barely audible, "My water just broke."

Trent's anger turned into disbelief as he stared at the wet spot steadily getting bigger on his floor.

"You have to take me to the hospital," she managed to say in between the contractions that were now beginning. "I can't have my baby standing here in your living room. Please baby, please help me," she begged.

Trent wasn't a mean-spirited guy and he still didn't know if the baby was his or not, there was a fifty-fifty chance that it was. Scooping Phylicia up into his arms, he carried her down to his car and drove her to the hospital without saying one word.

***

It had been a whole month since he'd found out that Phylicia was married and a month since she'd had the baby. A month since everything in his life had failed to have significance after that. Glancing around his condo, Trent knew that it was time for a change. He had to relocate. His whole apartment reminded him of Phylicia. Flopping into the chair in his room, he ran his hands down his face. *The baby isn't yours.* He could still hear the doctor's voice telling him. Phylicia's baby girl belonged to her husband. The betrayal was real. Phylicia was a fraud and he would never be able to forget or forgive her for any of this. He'd never trust another woman in his life. *To hell with them.* He thought as he grabbed his cell phone to dial his realtor. It was time for a move; he was putting his condo on the market. A fresh start for a new life is exactly what the doctor ordered and what he definitely needed.

***

Natalia was all smiles these days. She had just graduated Magna Cum Laude from NYU and couldn't be happier.

"You looked so good up there." Shay exclaimed at Natalia's apartment, giving her a hug. "I can't believe Erikka didn't come back for your graduation. I would have thought for sure she would have flown back for this."

Natalia laughed, "You know how E is, wanting to see the world and everything."

"I know it's been years, but it seems so weird that she up and left with no good-bye or anything."

"I was surprised as well. Shoot, I was living with her at the time. She never told me anything. Just one day I receive a postcard that says she wants to see the world and with every new place she goes, I get another postcard." Natalia lied. Not bothering to tell Shay that she would never see Erikka ever again.

"So what are your plans now?" Shay asked changing the subject letting the Erikka topic drop.

"I haven't narrowed it down yet, but I'll think of something."

"Ok, well keep me posted," she gave Natalia a kiss on the head, "I have to roll. I love you."

"Love you too." Natalia said as Shay exited her apartment.

Sitting down at her desk Natalia smiled when she saw the copies of Phylicia's marriage certificate on her desk. Phylicia had no idea who she was because she had yet to see her, but Natalia knew everything about Phylicia and she was going to use that to her advantage. She'd seen Phylicia move out of Trent's condo and knew that it was over between those two. Now it was her time and she meant to have it. Throwing on some street clothes, Natalia ran out to catch the train uptown.

***

Trent was packing the last of his things in boxes. His realtor had found him a nice new spot on 71st street and he was anxious to be settled in. It was seven-thirty in the morning. Kodi said that he would arrive around eight, so Trent had a half-hour to kill. The knock on the door was a welcome distraction from his roaming thoughts on Phylicia.

Looking through the peephole, Trent groaned.

"What's up Natalia?" He asked when he opened the door.

"Long time no hear from. You missed my graduation today." Natalia accused him marching into his condo, "I sent you an invitation."

"Yeah, I've been sorta busy." Trent glanced at Natalia shaking his head. It was a long time since he'd seen her, felt like a lifetime ago.

"You're moving?" Natalia stated in shock.

"Yup. Turning in my keys today."

"But why?"

"I need a change of scenery." Trent leaned up against the bare wall and studied her. "What can I do for you though?" He was curious as to why after he'd told Natalia to stay out of his life that almost two years later she happens to show up on his doorstep the day before he moves. The odds of the happening were unbelievable to him.

"I just wanted to check up on you and see how you were." Natalia told him with sincerity present in her voice.

"Ok. I'm good. You've seen me." Trent told her, not really up to her shenanigans today.

"Can I ask you a question?" Natalia asked looking up at him with soft inviting eyes, trying to entice him, it seemed. What she failed to realize was that he was immune to her.

"I guess," he shrugged.

"Why her?"

"Excuse me?" Trent asked confused.

"Why her?" That woman who you let move in. What made you; *Mr. No relationship* commit to her and not me?"

Trent drew a deep breath. It was too early in the morning for this type of heavy conversation.

"Did you hear me?" She pressed him.

"Yes Natalia," Trent responded in a bored slow tone, "I heard you."

"No answer?"

"What do you want me to say? That she was perfect for me. That she was my ideal woman. She was all those things and more," he threw his hands up in exasperation, frustrated and irritated with her intrusion in his life.

Natalia felt as if a blade had penetrated her heart.

"Perfect," she whispered, "You thought she was perfect why?" Her voice was laced with hurt.

"Because," Trent decided it was time to be honest with Natalia so that hopefully she would get the message that he no longer wanted anything to do with her and that she wasn't the woman for him. He needed to hurt her the only way he knew how, by professing his love and admiration for another woman, "To me; she could do anything. My personal super woman. Her heart spoke to mine. The day I met her, I knew I had to have her. All of her needed to belong to me and I wouldn't be satisfied until I had all of her." Trent told Natalia, not holding anything back. "I loved her. Still do, it just wasn't meant for us to be."

"What about me?" Natalia asked.

Trent blinked to refocus his thoughts on Natalia and to forget Phylicia.

"What about you?" Trent asked with nonchalance in his voice. "You weren't for me. You're young and naïve. Just a girl. I needed a woman and I found her."

"Well if she was so great, where is she now?" Natalia taunted.

"That's none of your concern. Why are you here?" Trent asked angrily.

"Because I love you and you know, deep down, that we are meant to be together."

"Don't you think if it were meant to be, it would be by now?" He asked her, "Let it go, Natalia. We've been done for years. I've moved on with my life. You should do the same."

"But it doesn't have to be that way," she whined, "I can be the woman you need me to be."

"I know you wish that were true." Trent told her sadly, "But that's not what it is. You have proven repeatedly to me that we are not compatible. That's just the way that it is. There is no me and you and there will be no me and you. You get it?" He needed her to know that he was serious and to move on with her life.

Natalia slowly nodded her head. "Yup, I got it," she said solemnly as she left the condo. Trent locked the door behind her when she left. Kodi couldn't show up soon enough. He was ready to move and be done with this place once and for all.

THE
PRESENT

Chapter 8

"Hi, baby." I was missing you." Trent smiled immediately
when he entered the house and saw Shia walking over to
him. He loved his wife. Shia always had the place glowing like
the sunshine just by her presence.

"Yo, what's good? I missed you, too." He bent down and
kissed her passionately on the lips.

"What have you been up to all day?"

Trent debated about telling her a lie or sticking with the truth.

"Just came back from visiting Phylicia."

Shia's animated face immediately crumbled. "Why would you do something like that?" she asked with a hint of attitude apparent in her voice as she stepped away from him. For the life of her, she couldn't understand why Trent would entertain going to see Phylicia. She had made their lives a living hell. Trent walked with a limp because she had tried to kill him. She understood the two of them had a past, but she wanted him to leave her where she belonged…in the past.

Trent grabbed her arms firmly but didn't apply too much pressure, just enough to get her to stop and look at him.

"I needed to go for me," he stared down into her eyes hoping that she would be able to understand. "I needed to forgive her about everything. Khloe, William, Sherri, me, you, your sisters," he paused, "All of it."

Shia stared into Trent's loving eyes and her attitude disintegrated. She knew he'd been fighting those Phylicia demons for years. Therefore, if seeing her allowed him peace of mind, then she could understand and accept that.

Rising on her tiptoes, Shia gently kissed Trent on the cheek.

"Are you feeling better now?" she asked him.

"Somewhat." Trent said sitting down on their leather, chestnut, brown sectional.

Shia sat next to him and pulled his head into her lap. Stroking the waves in his hair, she waited patiently as he continued his story.

Trent sighed, "I thought three years would be enough time for her to face her issues as well, but she's still the same old Phylicia, though she does regret killing Khloe, but that's about it."

Shia continued to stroke her husband's hair.

"Babe, you have to realize that Phylicia is a special head case, but she is who she is. Her love for you outshone her judgment. You can't fix her." Shia said leaning down to gently kiss him on the forehead, "She's going to have to want to fix herself."

"I know, but a part of me feels like it's my fault. She used to be the most perfect woman in the world to me."

Shia flinched a little when she heard those words. She knew Trent was only venting, but hearing it still wounded, even if only a little. No woman wanted to hear her husband say that another woman was perfect for him, even if it was someone from his past and she was the one with the ring and his last name.

"But after meeting you, "Trent went on, "I finally knew that what I and Phylicia had was never on the level of what you and I have now."

Shia smiled softly at Trent's words. She thanked God for her husband because he was the absolute best.

"Mom!"

Shia closed her eyes loathe to have the intimate time with her husband interrupted, but mommy duties called.

Trent sat up and watched as the twins entered the room. "Yes?"

"Guess what happened today!"

"Tell me." Shia replied with a smile.

"We both made the basketball team."

"You did! That's so amazing!" Shia beamed at them. At six, they were so handsome. She couldn't believe how big they had gotten so fast.

"That's great guys." Trent chimed in. Shia smiled. She was so grateful for Trent. Even though Trent wasn't the twin's biological father, he did a great job with the boys. He had taken over father duties immediately when he and Shia decided to make their thing deeper and their dad had been murdered.

"Gimmie hugs you two."

The boys ran over and enveloped Shia into a big hug. "Okay go change your clothes, dinner will be ready soon."

"Yes, ma'am," They said in unison as they exited the family room.

Kissing Trent on the lips Shia rose off the sectional. "You hungry?" she asked him.

Trent shook his head. "Nah, I think I'm a go out for a while. The guys at the job heading to the bar soon."

"Okay. Don't stay out too late." Shia said bending down to give him a hug and kiss before she retreated to the kitchen. "I love you."

"I won't and I love you, too."

***

"Shy, where is Trent?"

"What you all in my business for?" Shia asked Leigh smugly. Leigh had come over after getting off work, which was her normal routine every night.

Leigh rolled her eyes. "Your business is my business. Your man ain't never here when I come over."

"Maybe he's avoiding you." Shia smirked at her, "You ever think about that?"

"Ha, ha, very funny."

"Maybe if you got your own man you wouldn't be worried about mine all the time." Shia told her.

"Touche', my lovely twin, touché." Leigh laughed.

Shia handed Leigh a plate of fajita fixin's from the Mexican dinner she had prepared and sat down at the kitchen table.

"How *is* that area of your life going?"

Leigh sighed as she joined Shia at the table and began piling her fajita ingredients onto the tortilla.

"It's okay I guess." Leigh said taking a bite.

"Why just okay? Ever since I moved you don't talk to me as much."

Leigh swallowed her food.

"Yeah, I know. You off doing the family thing now and I try not to interrupt."

"Hey, you're my family, too." Shia said gazing at her through empathetic eyes. "Closer even, we're twins; we have a bond that no one can break. So tell your big sis what's going on."

"Girl, please." Leigh laughed. "You're only a big sis by three minutes. Let you tell it people would think that we were years apart."

Shia laughed, "So what. It counts." Shia made the laughter vanish from her voice and face, "But seriously Lei Lei, don't you want to share your life with somebody?" She asked her.

"Yeah, of course I do, but no one is running to my door trying to knock it down." Leigh shrugged indifferently. "I mean, there is this one guy Tyrique that I have been kind of kicking it with, but I don't really trust anyone after Kodi. I know that the Kodi situation was years ago, but guys run too many games. I can't keep up and don't want to play." Leigh told Shia. She remembered all too well the drama she'd been caught up in with her infatuation with Kodi, who had still been dealing with his son's mother Sherri and all the fights and hospital visits. Ever since those times, Leigh kept her distance from men. She wasn't skilled enough at the game to know who was being serious and who was running game because of that she had spent the last few years alone trying to work things out within herself. She had met Tyrique recently and he seemed interested, so she was going to attempt to see how it went but she was determined to try to take it as slow as possible.

"Ooh Tyrique." Shia said, "Very encouraging. Who's this?" Shia asked, giving Leigh her undivided attention.

Leigh shook her head and gave a little laugh, "Shy, don't start okay. It's nothing serious, just something to do."

"Okay." Shia said not wanting to push. She knew how Leigh felt about the whole dating thing. The fact that she even mentioned Tyrique said a lot. "Well I'm happy that you found something to do. I have never seen anyone hold on to someone as long as you did Kodi. That can't be healthy."

"I did not hold on to Kodi." Leigh replied indignantly.

Shia looked at Leigh as if to say *stop playing* with her facial expression.

"Okay, okay." Leigh laughed giving in, "I may have held on to him a little longer than necessary."

"Waaaaaaay longer than necessary. Like about eight years too long." Shia exaggerated. "But I'm happy that you are taking this step. I'm really proud of you."

"Aight Shy, leave me alone." Leigh laughed.

"So tell me about Tyrique." Shia asked deciding to drop the Kodi topic. "Where'd you meet him?" She asked curiously.

Leigh shrugged, "Out and about. Nothing exciting."

"Come on we're bonding here." Shia laughed pressing her a little. Leigh has been always so secretive. In order to get a direct answer, you had to ask a direct question and then ask it repeatedly until she felt backed into a corner to respond.

"You've gotten so bossy with your old age, since you're older than me and all." Leigh smirked as she winked at her.

Shia burst into laughter, "Girl will you stop stalling and spit it out?" Shia said shaking her head. Talking to Leigh was like pulling teeth.

"Seriously Shy, it was nothing exciting. My friend Shay and I were at Penn Station waiting for the E train and he approached me on the platform."

"Okay." Shia said nodding her head up and down. "There's nothing wrong with that. That's actually very normal. I'm just so happy that you finally meet someone and are dating again. I was worried that you had let that whole Kodi thing ruin you."

"Dating isn't the part that worries me, it's the trusting part. Look at what you went through with Demetri as well."

Shia moved concerned eyes to meet Leigh's sad ones. She knew all too well how tough it was to trust men, her deceased husband Demetri had taken their family through so much trying to seek revenge on some old grudge with their mother. Shia decided to leave the topic alone altogether.

"Are you lonely in that apartment without Remi?"

Leigh shrugged grateful for the shift in conversation, "It's different. I miss her, but I understand, after everything that went on with our family and especially with the things that were done to her, she needed to get away. Miami is the perfect place for her. She's such a party girl."

"I agree." Shia knew all too well all the demons that the sisters struggled with, but Remi's cut very deep. The daily rapes from Shia's husband, Demetri had taken a toll on her. Shia had asked her to go to counseling and find a way to deal with it, but

Remi had wanted to deal with it in her own way. Shia refocused her attention on Leigh and studied her for a moment, "You sure you're okay, Lei Lei?"

"I'm alright, Shy. I promise." Leigh replied as she continued to eat her food.

Shia was silent for a moment before she spoke softly. "Trent went to visit Phylicia today."

Leigh stopped chewing and stared at Shia in exaggerated horror, "Are you serious? What did he visit that loony skank for?" Leigh exclaimed.

"I believe it was so he could rest easy. He's been battling Phylicia issues for so long. I think it was more a closure piece for him."

"Really?" Leigh asked as she resumed her chewing, "How do you feel about that?"

Shia sighed lightly, "I just want him to be happy. If that's what he needed to do to find peace. Then so be it."

"Shy you are such a good wife because I would have lost it with that one. I don't see how you do it."

"I have no reason to lose it. Phylicia doesn't have anything on me. She's stuck in a mentally insane hospital for who knows how many years. I'm not wasting my time going crazy over her."

"So what did you bring it up for?"

"Because something is wrong. I can feel it in my core. I don't know how or what, but something isn't sitting right with me. I keep waking up out my sleep in cold sweats feeling like something is about to happen or had happened. Something just isn't right."

"And you think Phylicia has something to do with it?" Leigh's voice had disbelief etched into it. "Shy, Phylicia is put away, just as you pointed out a second ago. She couldn't possibly be doing anything to you."

"I know it sounds silly, but I'm telling you Leigh, something just isn't right." Shia knew her twin probably thought she was losing her mind, but she knew what she was feeling was real.

"Have you talked to Trent about this?"

Shia shook her head no, as she watched her and Trent's three-year-old daughter Joelle run into the kitchen playing with her ball, Shia knew her hunch wasn't wrong.

"No I don't want to bother him. What if it turns out to be nothing?"

"But, what if it turns out to be everything?" Leigh asked, concerned for her sister.

***

"Yo T! You want another shot?"

"Yeah, one more is cool." Trent replied. He was enjoying his time out at the bar with his co-workers. Sometimes he needed this release. Not that he hated going home or anything because he felt like he had the best wife in the world. He just needed some down time with someone besides the family every once in a while, which is why he hung out with his co-workers from time to time, just to have something else to do. When his homeboy Kodi killed himself, Trent lost the closest thing that he had to a brother and now he was left trying to figure everything out for himself. He wondered why things had to turn out the way they did and what he could have done differently to stop so many of the past events from happening. He had finally come to terms with the fact that he was angry with Kodi for killing himself. That was something he hadn't expected from his friend. He'd expected him to fight through it until the end. Trent finally had come to terms with what he was feeling. He was angry with Kodi for taking the cowardly way out of the situation instead of dealing with it head on. Picking up the shot that was set in front of him, Trent threw it back and tried to forget about his problems for a while.

***

She watched the sisters from her binoculars as they engaged in chatter over dinner. The house had been bugged for weeks and she had been listening to their conversations trying to get any information that she could. Lowering the binoculars, she watched as Trent parked in front of the house and went inside.

Lifting the binoculars back up, she watched as Trent walked over and kissed Shia before exiting the kitchen and heading to the master bedroom.

"Pumpkin, it's time for you to get going. I have plans to seduce my husband."

"Geez, just push me out the house why don't you. I can take a hint, as subtle as it was."

She grinned at the twins' conversation and watched as they both stood, hugged and Leigh exited the house.

Eyes following Leigh's disappearing headlights, then she quickly returned necessary attention to the house watching as Shia kissed her twin boys goodnight, then went into her daughter's room and read her a story before putting her to bed as well.

Continuing to watch as Shia entered the master bedroom joining her husband; she lowered the audio on her earpiece and laid her binoculars down not wanting to listen to the sounds or see the act of the couple's lovemaking. When the couple finally laid to rest, she watched another hour before calling it a night. She would return in time for the couple's start of the day in a few hours.

***

Shia sat upright in bed, not sure what had awoken her. She and Trent had only gone to bed an hour ago after a pleasurable night of showing each other love the best way they knew how.

Looking around the room uneasily, Shia had an unsettling feeling. Something was wrong somewhere. Lying back down next to a sleeping Trent, she sighed in contentment when he reached for her while still sleeping and pulled her close. Shia closed her eyes as she relaxed against her husband's warm body hoping to keep the uneasiness away.

The next morning, Shia rose before the rest of her family after a night of restlessness. Kissing her husband on the forehead, she went down the hall to check on their children. All of them were sound asleep. She smiled before retreating downstairs to get breakfast started before she had to get them up and send them to school.

Later that day at her office at the Museum of Modern Art where she had been an art buyer for the past few years, Shia kept getting a sense that she was being watched. Glancing around her office, everyone seemed to be milling about doing normal day-to-day activities. The normal diva chick clique was at the water cooler checking out the same men they checked out every day, as if something new and fabulous had changed with them. The no nonsense overachiever group was doing what they do best with their heads buried in their computer screens. There was one new girl, but she didn't speak to anyone, very secretive. All Shia knew was that her name was Richele Bynes. Shia kept her distance from her though, not because she didn't like her, but because she wasn't in the mood to make any new friends.

Shia's desk phone buzzed.

"Yes?" She said into the receiver.

"Your husband is here."

Shia smiled instantly. She loved when Trent surprised her at work.

Walking through her office with a bouquet of Calla lilies, her favorite flowers, and a bag from Cosi her favorite deli spot, Shia thought he'd never looked so handsome.

The diva chick clique's eyes all turned to Trent as he made his way toward her. She could see the envy on their faces. Beaming a toothy smile in their direction, she French-kissed her husband, taking him off guard when he had originally leaned down for a peck.

"Don't get something started in your office. I don't think your coworkers would take too kindly to seeing your ass up in the air while I tapped it on your desk." Trent whispered into her ear so that no one in the office could hear.

Shia laughed as she removed the bouquet from his hands.

"This is a nice surprise," she told him shutting her office door; blocking out the haters.

Trent took a seat in one of the chairs in front of her desk.

"I was missing my wife," he said seductively.

"Good. You should always miss your wife." Shia smiled, "Thanks for coming and bringing lunch. You are the absolute greatest husband ever and I love you."

"I love you." Trent responded.

"I'm glad you came, you brightened my whole mood today. I've been thinking about taking some time off or looking for another job. I'm over this place."

"What seems to be the problem?" Trent asked taking a bite of his turkey and Brie sandwich.

"Same ole, same ole I think I may just need a change of scenery. The women here are so catty and the woman who just started she's a little weird; keeps to herself." Trent turned to look out her office window into the common area.

"Yeah, which one?"

Shia glanced at Richele's desk and saw that she was no longer sitting there. "She may have gone to lunch, but she's really secretive and weird." Shia summed it up.

"As long as it doesn't rub off on my Mami, then it's cool."

"Oh hush." Shia laughed as she and Trent continued to enjoy their lunch together. "I think I really want to just spend more time at home with Joelle and maybe expanding our family. How do you feel about that?"

"Whatever you want to do is fine with me. I look forward to all the practice that we'll get working on the expansion." Trent smirked as he took another bite of his sandwich.

Shia laughed, "Oh, I bet you will," she told him grateful that he had taken time to eat lunch with her today.

Chapter 9

A *nother day has passed.* She thought as she opened her eyes and heard the hospital staff making their morning rounds. She quickly shut her eyelids when a staff member came close to her bunk.

"Alright Ms. Phylicia, I know you heard me coming, open those eyes it's time for your meds."

Phylicia kept her eyes closed and refused to budge.

"So, this is the type of day you're choosing to have?" The staff member took a deep breath, "Ok it's your choice," she said in a singsong voice, "I'll let the Director know."

Phylicia's eyes popped open.

"I'm up for goodness. Give me the drugs."

The staff member smiled at her, "Glad to see that you changed your mind," she handed Phylicia a small Dixie cup with three small white pills inside.

Snatching the little cup from her hands, Phylicia tipped the cup up to her mouth and allowed the three pills to hit her tongue, handing the cup back to the staff member whose nametag read Lily Tate. Phylicia almost threw up in disgust. *Lily* how appropriate she thought as she gazed at the woman who looked like she belonged down on a farm.

"Good girl." Lily took the cup from Phylicia's hands and handed her a plastic cup filled with water.

Rolling her eyes, Phylicia accepted the water-filled cup and quickly took a sip before handing it back to Lily.

Lily stood there expectedly as Phylicia opened her mouth lifting her tongue to show that she had swallowed the pills. Satisfied, Lily moved on to the next room.

Making sure Lily wasn't looking, Phylicia swiftly removed the pills that had hidden on the back of her mouth between her gums, and cheek out her mouth and into an envelope that she kept folded under the bedpost.

The staff thought they were slick by keeping everyone medicated, so that they would remain subdued, but Phylicia was hip to their system and wasn't having it.

***

"Mail call." The male attendant shouted from the hall.

Phylicia stood slowly to her feet as a small envelope was pushed under her door. Reaching down to retrieve the envelope from off the floor, she slowly opened the envelope flap that neglected to have any postage or return address on it and read the handwritten letter inside.

I admire you.

Phylicia frowned at the unassigned letter as she flipped it over looking for a clue as to who could have written it. Who would admire me? She thought. Placing the letter on the side table next to her bed, Phylicia put the letter out of her mind for the time being. Being stuck in the psych ward for the past four years she wanted out, but her thoughts would have to wait. Looking up as her room door opened, she walked toward the door. That was the signal that it was time for dinner.

***

After dinner, Phylicia was shocked to see another letter placed upright on her pillow when she got back to her room. Moving swiftly toward her bed, Phylicia sat on her comforter and eyed the envelope with her name written delicately across the front intently. Her name was written in the same neat handwriting as the envelope she had received earlier that day.

Tracing the letters of her name on the envelope with the tip of her fingernail, she squinted her eyes wondering if someone was attempting to play a joke on her.

After a few more minutes of staring at the foreign envelope on her pillow, she picked it up and opened it.

You are my idol. I admire you and your work. Will tell you more this evening. Midnight. Wait for the sign.

Phylicia put the letter down on top of the first one she'd received that was lying on her side table. Like the first letter, this one wasn't signed either. Glancing at the round, plastic clock on the wall the time reflected eight PM, and deciding to go to sleep, she laid down to catch a nap so that she could be awake and alert by midnight. To see what this mysterious sign would be.

Phylicia woke with a jolt as a soft clicking of the door easing open seeped into her consciousness. She sat up and watched as an unfamiliar male entered the room holding a finger to his lips indicating that Phylicia should stay silent.

"I'm going to get you out of here." The male whispered to Phylicia as he handed her a worker's jacket that matched his and a black bob wig.

Phylicia gazed at him skeptically not accepting the jacket or wig. Everything about this felt like a setup.

"You're going to have to trust me." The man said, practically shoving the jacket and wig into Phylicia's arms. "We have to move fast. Come on!" He said in an urgent tone.

Phylicia weighed the pros and cons. She could either stay in the mental hospital until the judge and doctors decided to let her out, to which she had no idea of the timeline, or she could follow this man, free herself of this place, and deal with the strange guy later.

Taking the items from the man, Phylicia quickly downed them since time was of the essence.

"Ok, let's go." The man said once Phylicia was ready. Walking over to the table, Phylicia grabbed the letter and put them into her jacket pocket then moved quickly toward the door.

"When we get in the hall stay close to my side and if someone comes let me do all the talking. "Okay?" The man asked eyeing Phylicia intently.

Phylicia nodded her head in acknowledgment and followed the man as they exited the room that had housed her and had been her home for the past four years.

Sticking close to the man, the two swiftly made their way down the hall towards the exit. They came to an electric gate. The man punched a code into the keypad next to the gate, and it unlocked.

"Almost out," he whispered as he turned a corner and continued down another hall.

Phylicia's adrenaline was flowing rapidly now. The realization that she was about to be free began to set in and she was becoming anxious to clear the security gate. She was interested in seeing how the man was going to get her past that point without getting them found out.

When the duo reached the security desk, Phylicia was surprised to see the security desk empty. Thus, making their escape that much easier. Phylicia couldn't believe their good fortune as the man keyed in another code for the exit gate and the gate opened to free them from the facility.

Breathing in the fresh air, Phylicia was astonished by how easy it had been for her to escape. She glanced over at the man who had orchestrated her escape and wondered who he was and what he wanted.

"Who are you?"

"Not here." The man answered, "When we're in the clear I'll tell you everything you need to know. My car is over here," he pointed at an all-black Audi sitting on twenty-inch black on black rims.

Pulling out his car keys, he pressed the key pad, and the car lights flashed twice indicating that the doors were unlocked and ready.

"Come on. Let's get out of here," the man said, sliding behind the wheel.

Phylicia entered the car on the passenger side and snapped her seatbelt into place. Unsure of what to think of the caramel skinned man sitting next to her exiting the parking lot of the hospital.

"They'll be looking for me, you do know that?" Phylicia said to him, "Which means that they will be looking for you as well."

"I've got it all covered. They'll never catch me." The mystery man replied to Phylicia as he drove on in silence for about twenty minutes before pulling up to the Port Authority on 42nd street. "This is your stop."

"What?" Phylicia looked at the man as if he were the crazy one.

The man pointed to a black unmarked van parked on the corner.

"There in that van is the answer to all your questions." Giving Phylicia a look of admiration, he drew her in for a hug. "Such a pleasure to meet you finally."

Phylicia returned the hug in confused silence. She wasn't worried because she could hold her own if something popped off with this strange man, but she stayed on her guard just in case.

Drawing back from the embrace, the man pulled a 9mm out from under the driver seat.

"You may need this," he said handing the weapon to Phylicia along with a box of ammunition.

Eyeing him warily, Phylicia received the machinery with ease. She felt more comfortable now that she was fully armed and prepared.

"Go." The man nodded toward the van. "She's waiting for you."

"Thank you." Phylicia whispered while unbuckling her seatbelt and reaching for the door handle.

"It was my pleasure," were the last words Phylicia heard from the man before shutting the car door and jogging down to the black van sitting idly on the corner waiting for her arrival. The van door opened and Phylicia slid in. Once safely in, the van door closed and pulled out into traffic.

"Glad you could make it." A masked woman sitting in the back of the van commented.

"Who are you?" Phylicia asked.

"You'll see soon enough." The masked woman said as the van forged ahead and they rode in silence until they reached their destination, a brownstone sitting in a quiet neighborhood in Jersey.

Phylicia narrowed her eyes when they pulled up in front of the house. "Where are we?"

"Come on in, so that you can find out." The woman said to her as she got out of the van and waited for Phylicia to follow.

Phylicia exited the car at a slower pace; she wasn't too fond of all this anonymous business. She needed to know whom the woman was with and where they were, but she would bid her time and wait. If being locked away in the hospital had taught her nothing else, it had definitely taught her patience.

***

The last few hours were intense for Phylicia. Being broken out that god-awful hospital was the beginning of everything. The man who had broken her out had yet to resurface, but he was insignificant as far as Phylicia was concerned. The woman who mattered, the reason she was here in this brownstone was Natalia. Natalia was the one that had orchestrated her escape. Phylicia hadn't seen Natalia in years and she wondered what she could want from her. One thing that she knew was that she couldn't be trusted and Phylicia knew that she would do well to keep that in mind.

"I still can't believe you're here. You're my idol." Natalia spoke softly.

Phylicia flashed a bright smile. However, she was grateful for Natalia breaking her out; that didn't mean that she believed anything coming out of her mouth because nothing was free. Phylicia was waiting to see what Natalia wanted in return.

"I was thinking we could team up. The two of us could do a----.

"I work alone." Phylicia replied cutting her off. Natalia narrowed her eyes slightly, but refused to be so easily deterred.

"But we could shut things down." Natalia was amped and ready.

"I don't need help with that." Phylicia stood up, "Look, I appreciate what you did for me," she paused, "I'm not really sure why you did, but I really need to get going."

"I could make it worth your while." Natalia taunted.

Natalia paused for emphasis, raising her eyebrows slightly. "I know where Trent and Shia live with their children."

That statement halted Phylicia in her tracks as she gazed at Natalia in a new light. Maybe she could be beneficial to her after all, what Phylicia really wanted to know was how she knew about she and Trent.

"How do you know about that?" She asked perplexed giving Natalia her undivided attention.

"I know everything about you." Natalia's eyes aglow with admiration. "I idolize you." Natalia smiled a wicked grin at her. She had planned for this moment when Phylicia would be here for a long time. No deed went unpunished and Phylicia needed to be punished for so many things that Natalia was losing count, but her biggest grudge was Trent so she would start there. A little karma never hurt anyone and Phylicia's karma was about to get real.

Phylicia's eyes collided with Natalia's. She could see the wild side Natalia was trying to suppress, and Phylicia narrowed her eyes.

"Come. I want to show you something." Natalia said hopping out of her chair, grabbing Phylicia by the hand and pulling her to the back room that she kept sealed off from the rest of the house.

Once they were in the room Natalia released Phylicia's hand and flipped a switch on the far wall behind an Andy Warhol rendition painting of Marilyn Monroe. When she flipped the switch, the wall shifted back and displayed a set of stairs.

111

Phylicia followed Natalia, not trusting her for one minute; with her hand on the gun from the man had given her, just in case Natalia tried something funny and she had to put a hole between her eyes; as she began her decent down the stairs into a private cave-like room.

When Natalia turned on a light, Phylicia stopped moving in disbelief. The cave like room was littered with numerous photos of Phylicia from infancy until present day, one taken as recent as this morning as she had broken free of the mental institution.

"What is all this?" She whispered.

"My salute to you. I'm your biggest fan."

"Natalia cut the crap okay. You're not a fan of mine; I'm not buying it okay." Phylicia had finally had enough of whatever game Natalia was playing, "How did you get all these photos of me?"

Natalia shrugged. "I do my research."

"I see." Phylicia responded. Making a mental note to do her own background check on Natalia. As she looked around taking the room in, she noticed photos of Trent, Shia, their boys, and a baby girl.

"I followed your case when it was happening." Natalia's voice penetrated through Phylicia's psyche. "I saved all the newspaper clippings. Do you want to see them?" Phylicia heard Natalia ask.

Phylicia shook her head no continuing to stare at Trent's photo. The man who was the love of her life and had only checked on her one time.

"Ok," Phylicia turned to face Natalia. "Maybe we can entertain the idea of working together." Phylicia said without further hesitation. She watched as Natalia's eyes lit up like fireworks on the fourth of July. Phylicia knew that Natalia was up to something and Phylicia was going to make it a point to find out sooner than later, but she couldn't deny that Natalia had access to something she desperately wanted and that was Trent. So she would make it a point to stay on her guard, Natalia definitely wouldn't catch her slipping. Phylicia would play the game, but on her terms and she was going to make it a point to teach Natalia some lessons in the process if she thought that she could one up Phylicia at any moment.

"Before I decide, what information do you have on Trent and his family?" Phylicia asked her curious to see how much information Natalia really was working with.

"Plenty." Natalia replied sitting in a lone chair in the room, pulling out an accordion like folder filled with numerous files. "Where would you like to begin?"

Phylicia sat Indian-style on the cold floor next to Natalia so she could see the files clearly for herself.

"I'm not sure. Let me see what you have."

Natalia began handing the files over and Phylicia was in awe of the information before her. Natalia definitely did her research. Phylicia now was privy to Trent and Shia's address, where Shia's twins went to school, their phone numbers, where the two worked, the entire families' social security numbers, bank statements, stocks and investments. Where they spent their free time, the bar Trent went to with his social workers, Remi's address in Miami and where Leigh lived in New York as well.

"This is amazing." Phylicia eyed Natalia suspiciously. "Why are you doing this? What is it that you want from me?" She asked moving the files to the floor.

Natalia's lips spread into a slow wicked grin.

"To be your partner." She stated matter-of-factly, "Between the two of us, we could really do some damage."

"I don't usually work with partners." Phylicia told her again, as she pushed herself up off the floor. "Is this why you broke me out? Is that what your aim was," she looked at her with disbelief in her eyes, "Just to work with me?"

Phylicia narrowed her almond-shaped brown eyes as she stared into Natalia's light gray ones. "I know I agreed to work with you, but I was caught up in my mind on Trent, now that I'm thinking a little more clearly, why would I work with you? There is nothing you have that I could benefit from." Phylicia said intentionally baiting her to see what her response would be.

Natalia arched her eyebrow as she returned Phylicia's cool stare. The stakes were high, but she was ready to play Phylicia's game the way she played it.

"On the contrary, I have plenty you can benefit from." Natalia gestured toward the floor, "Maybe you would like to sit back down as you listen."

"I'll stand." Phylicia snapped back doing a quick eye sweep of the room for any potential weapons she could use against Natalia if it became necessary and she couldn't get to the gun she had tucked in her waistband fast enough. She stood and listened as Natalia forged ahead with the information that she had and what her plan of action was going to be.

Chapter 10

L eigh had to give it to Tyrique; he really was trying to court
her. They'd been dating for the past six months on the low.
It wasn't that Leigh was ashamed of Ty, but she wanted to
figure out where the situation was going before she had
mentioned anything about it to her sisters. Now that Shia had
coerced the information out of her, she prayed that everything
with her and Ty stayed good. She hadn't dealt with a man since
Kodi because of the range of emotions she knew she was

capable of feeling and how they made her act like a raving lunatic.

Removing the card from the Edible Arrangement fruit display that had just been delivered at her apartment, Leigh smiled. *You had to love a brother for trying,* she thought. A knock at the front door seized her attention away from the arrangement, now sitting on her kitchen counter. Standing on tiptoe to glance through the peephole, Leigh shook her head in amusement when she saw Ty on the other end whistling a tune.

"What are you doing here?" She asked him with a smile when she opened the door.

"Coming to see you," he said holding out a purple teddy bear with a heart in the middle that said *Teddy woves you* for her to take.

"Ty," she laughed, "What is all this?" She said taking the bear and stepping back so that he could enter her apartment.

"Just trying to brighten your day." Ty said removing his NY fitted cap and setting it on her wood coffee table as he took a seat in her chocolate and cream leather loveseat.

Sitting on the matching sofa across from Tyrique, Leigh smiled. "You have succeeded."

"What you got going on for today?" He asked her.

Leigh took him in and thought he looked very handsome laid back chillin' in her place. Tyrique had more of a gentle spirit about him. The complete opposite of Kodi. Kodi had never really been nice to her. She couldn't understand why she hung around following him and disrupting his life as long as she had.

He'd excited her at the time with his bad boy ways and antics. Now that she was older, she needed someone a little calmer and Ty offered her that.

Tyrique stood about 5'10 and God thought it fit to encase all 5'10" of him in chocolate and Leigh wasn't about to complain because she absolutely loved it. Reminding her of the actor Idris Elba, Leigh wasn't going to lie, she almost became putty in his hands from the first moment she saw him standing on the platform checking her out. She'd been interested, so she had been ecstatic when he'd come over to her and opened a conversation as if they were lifelong friends. She did enjoy that one quality about him. It felt like they had known each other forever. They were completely comfortable with each other.

"Nothing yet. It's raining out and I hate walking up and down New York streets in the rain." Leigh gazed at him inquiringly, "Why, did you want to do something?"

"Yeah. Chill with you," he said standing up and removing his windbreaker, "I'm not doing any design work today, so I have plenty of time."

"And how do you know that I don't have plans for the day?"

"You just told me you didn't." Ty's low laughter rose to her ears, "Which is why I didn't remove my jacket until you said that. I'm going to have to teach you to be more observant."

"Ok," Leigh responded in a laughing tone, "What are we supposed to do inside all day while the rain pours down outside?"

"I'm sure we could think of some things." Ty looked down at her sitting on the sofa and grinned.

"I bet you would like for us to do *"Some,"* things as you say."

"Relax. I just want to spend time with you and since I'm here and you're here let's do that and enjoy each other's company."

Leigh eyed him for a moment in silence, having an internal war with herself. Part of her wanted him to stay and chill with her. The other part of her wanted to run as fast as she could away from Tyrique. Even though he was different from Kodi, she still had a hard time trusting men. She liked Tyrique, but she was afraid of getting hurt again. Between her and Shia, they had more than their share of what could happen when you trusted a man too much.

"Have you and you worked it out yet?" He cracked a dry smile at her.

Leigh couldn't help but giggle. "Sort of. Me and me have decided that you can stay, but…" she paused and held up her pointer finger, "No funny business."

Ty nodded, "No funny business. Got it. Is it safe to ask you if you own a deck of cards?"

Leigh laughed as she stood up, "Who doesn't have cards. Of course I have some." Pulling out one of the drawers of her wooden entertainment stand, she fished the deck out and began to hand it to him. "I have to warn you though, holding the cards just outside his reach, "I am the queen at all card games. Not trying to toot my own horn or anything, but beep beep boo boo," she said laughing.

Ty joined her in laughter as he reached out and took the deck from her, "We'll see about that. Have a seat."

Two hours later and Leigh was freshly beaten to a pulp in every game they played from goldfish to tonk to two person spades, she'd lost them all.

"Now what were you saying? You're the Queen of what?" Ty taunted her in amusement.

Leigh's face broke into a Colgate grin, "I'm still the Queen, just not at cards with you so much," she laughed.

Tyrique put the cards on the table and leaned up grabbing her by her arms and dragging her into the love seat with him placing her firmly on top of his lap.

"You are my Queen." His deep voice whispered in her ear.

Leigh felt her body go into a full on blush and knew that he could see it.

"Don't get embarrassed. You know I like you," he told her. "Why do you think that I come over here all the time?"

"So you don't have to cook. You ain't fooling nobody." Leigh said playfully smacking him on the arm.

"Now that you say that, I am a little hungry."

"See," she smacked him harder on his arm this time, "There you go using me."

"I would never use you, but what you got to eat around here, or you going to let your man starve?"

When Leigh heard the words, *your man,* she froze in his arms. No man had ever wanted that title before. Kodi had run from even the thought of being with her as if she repulsed him.

Leigh tilted her head to look into his chestnut-brown eyes, "My man huh? You think you qualify."

Tyrique twisted his lips at her, "I'm over qualified Ma," he lifted her to her feet, "Now get in there, and fix your man something to eat," he said smacking her on the ass.

Leigh swatted his hand away and entered the kitchen rummaging through the cabinets and the refrigerator looking for something that would be quick to throw together.

"All I have are ingredients for a turkey and Swiss on Rye with honey mustard," she called out to him, "Is that okay?"

"It's cool." Tyrique said, looking down at his cell as it began to vibrate indicating that a text message was coming through. *All systems are a go. Meet us at the spot in an hour. More instructions will be given once you get there.* The message read. "Yo, can you make that to go. I gotta head out."

Leigh reentered the living room placing a sandwich in a Ziploc bag on the table, "You're out already?"

Tyrique stood up and kissed her on the forehead as he picked up the sandwich, "Duty calls. I'll hit you up later."

"Ok." Leigh said to his retreating as he exited her front door.

***

121

Tyrique did freelance design work and other odd jobs from time to time. This time he had an assignment to pick up and deliver a truck. That's all he knew. Heading to the junk yard where he was told the truck would be he waited for a signal.

"You here to pick up black?" an older white mechanic in dirty overall's and a toothpick hanging out his mouth asked him.

Tyrique nodded.

"Here are the keys. Put these gloves on before you touch these." Tyrique took the gloves the man handed him before he took the keys.

"She's over there." The mechanic said pointing to the back of the lot. Tyrique looked at the brand new Black Tahoe SUV and smiled. He loved new automobiles.

"Here are the instructions of what you're supposed to do?" The mechanic said handing him a folded piece of yellow paper.

Tyrique nodded yes.

"Good. Never come back here after this." The mechanic told him as he disappeared around the back.

Tyrique opened the door to the truck and pulled off. Glancing at the instructions in his hand, he broke out into a slight sweat. He hated the initiation process in anything, but he knew that he would be able to handle this assignment with ease as long as he didn't think about it too much and just focused on getting the job   done.

Chapter 11

Shia woke with a jolt out of her sleep. Forehead doused in sweat. She could tell that something wasn't right. Sitting up slowly in the bed she turned her head and her tension eased and face relaxed once she saw Trent sleeping and resting easy next to her.

Leaning down, she softly placed a kiss on his eyebrow and quietly rose out the bed. Removing her silk robe from the side chair, Shia put it on and headed out the bedroom she and Trent shared.

Walking down the hall Shia went into the nursery and glanced into the toddler bed. Her heart melted as she watched her tiny tot's chest rise and fall with each breath. She found it hard to believe that Joelle was getting so big so fast, seemed like just yesterday she had been born. Smiling at the bittersweet memory, Shia turned and tiptoed out the room not wanting to disturb Joelle. She may have been angelic while sleeping, but awake she was a terror on chubby legs.

Moving down the hall, she opened the door to the twin's room and was satisfied that they were asleep as well. Closing the door behind her as she exited the room, she couldn't shake the nagging feeling that something somewhere was very wrong.

Silently making her way down the stairs, Shia entered the living room and laid across the cream leather sectional that she loved to fall into. Grabbing the remote, she clicked on the 71 inch Vizio Cinema wide LCD TV that Trent just had to have.

Sighing as the NY1 news station emerged into view, she couldn't understand why Trent insisted on watching the news all the time. All they ever showed were the bad things happening all around them and frankly, she found it very depressing.

Shia watched as the newscasters went over the usual crime and violence in the area, and then sat up when a breaking news bulletin came across the screen. "Alert-Breakout at the local hospital for the criminally insane. Phylicia Lynn Taylor has escaped. Shia gazed at the screen in horror as a mug shot of Phylicia appeared on the screen.

Leaping up off the sectional Shia ran to the front door to check the locks and ran back to the living room to finish watching the news report.

"Phylicia is known to be dangerous. With her whereabouts unknown, we are asking if you see this woman to notify the local authorities as soon as possible. Thank you."

The screen quickly switched to the weather report and Shia suddenly felt as if she and her family were completely exposed. Walking over and shutting the television off. Shia knew she wouldn't have to wonder where Phylicia was for long. As sure as she knew the sun rose and set, she was sure Phylicia would be making her presence known to them sooner than later and who knew what she would be capable of this time around.

"Baby wake up." Shia spoke lowly to Trent when she reentered their bedroom.

"Hhmm," he mumbled as he lifted his arm attempting to draw her in close to him without opening his eyes.

Shia gently pulled just outside his reach. "No baby, wake up please." Leaning down kissing his chest, she felt him begin to stir.

"Why you playing, but obviously not going to give me any," he said groggily without opening his eyes.

"Because I need you to focus. I promise to give you some later if you get up and listen to me."

Trent sat up slowly, looking completely disoriented. Shia thought he looked absolutely adorable, shirtless letting his muscles ripple.

"What's so important that I need to get up in the middle of the night and focus on, that's more important than me getting some from my wife." Trent asked scratching his head; yawning.

"Phylicia escaped." Shia said trying to keep herself from going into a frantic panic.

That statement broke the rest of Trent's sleepiness. He was now fully awake and focused.

"You sure?"

"Yes. It was on the news. They don't know where she is."

Trent's cell phone ringing broke the stillness of the night. Throwing off the bed covers, he stood to retrieve his phone and saw an unknown number calling.

"Hello."

"This is the FBI. We have units on the way to your house right now to place your family in protective custody."

"That won't be necessary."

"You're refusing protection. You are aware that Ms. Taylor is Free?" The agent asked.

"Yes, my family and I are aware. Thank you." Trent replied hanging up the phone.

"What was that about?" Shia asked.

"The FBI is trying to offer us protection from Phylicia."

"And you don't think we need it?" Shia asked skeptically. She was trying her hardest not to go into hysterics, but Trent seemed to be taking this whole situation a little too lightly for her.

"Shia we'll be okay. I'll protect you and my family at all costs."

"You promise?" Shia whispered, "You know how deranged Phylicia is."

Trent kissed Shia's pouty lips. "Trust me." I met with her."

"I know, but you told me that she hadn't changed. My question to you is that if she hasn't changed why do you think that we are safe? I need some reassurance here."

Trent could see that Shia was on edge and he wanted to ease her fears, but he honestly did think that Phylicia wasn't out to harm them in any way. He knew that she loved him and wouldn't hurt him unless she was cornered.

"I'm trying to reassure you, just trust what I'm telling you. She won't hurt me."

"It's not just you I'm worried about per se. I'm thinking about the children and me my sisters, all of those things. She doesn't love us. I mean she killed her own daughter, do you honestly think that she will spare us?"

"You have to trust me Babe." Trent said trying to do his best to reassure her.

"I do trust you, but I'm worried." Shia stated plainly.

"Everything will be fine. I promise."

"Okay." Shia said hesitantly, "I believe you."

***

"Baby, you want me to pick something up for you to eat when I go get the twins?" Shia shouted out the window to Trent who was taking a break from cutting the grass.

"Yes, babe. That would be great." Taking a quick guzzle of water from the ice-cold bottle Shia had left on the deck for him, he took a rag out of his pocket to wipe the sweat from his face.

Shia continued to stare at Trent for several minutes after he had answered her question. She adored her husband and still couldn't believe that he had chosen her as his wife with his handsome self. After all these years, he was still gorgeous to her and she loved him with everything that she had in her.

"When the smoke clears, we dry our tears…Only in Love and War." Shia sang at the top of her lungs to Tamar Braxton's song. Shia still rocked to it as if it was brand new. She always enjoyed her alone time when she had to get the twins. So engrossed in her song she didn't see the black truck flying straight toward her until it was too late to react.

"OH NO!" Shia screamed as her car and the truck collided head on into one another smashing both vehicles into accordions.

***

"Daddy look!" Joelle squealed as she jumped up and down in excitement pointing at something in the grass.

Trent instantly smiled as he walked over to his daughter and bent down to see what had caught her undivided attention in the dirt. He enjoyed these moments when the two of them could just enjoy Daddy, daughter time.

"It's a worm." Trent said picking the worm up and placing it in his hand so Joelle could get a better look at it. "You want to hold it?"

"No." Joelle said shaking her head as she stood next to him eyeing the worm suspiciously, as if she didn't trust it not to jump on her.

"It won't hurt you." Trent tried unsuccessfully to convince Joelle otherwise, but she was having none of it.

"No Daddy, No!" she said then ran off jumping and playing in the other direction. No longer interested in him or the worm. Trent laughed lowly as he put the worm back in the grass. Shaking his head at the attention span of three-year olds.

After allowing Joelle to play outside for another half hour, he took her in her house to clean her up for dinner.

Trent placed a small plastic bowl in front of Joelle sitting in her chair, before glancing at his watch wondering what was taking Shia so long.

"Mmm Daddy. It's good."

Trent smiled at Joelle, "Gobble it up princess," he said moving to the refrigerator to prepare dinner for the rest of the family when he was interrupted the phone ringing.

Taking a quick peek at Joelle to make sure she was good, Trent answered the wall phone in the kitchen.

"Hello?"

"Trent." Leigh's hysterical voice came across the line, "Shy has been in an accident."

"What!" Trent shouted into the phone.

"They need you to get to the hospital."

"Ok. I'm on my way. Is she okay?"

"I'm not certain. They wouldn't give me any info over the phone. I'm going to get the boys."

Trent shut his eyes, mind reeling. "Okay, okay. I'm headed there now. What hospital?"

"Mount Sinai."

Trent felt as if Mike Tyson himself in his heyday had gut punched him because his lungs seemed to be failing him.

"Okay. I'll see you there," he hung up.

"Finished Daddy!" Joelle squealed from her chair at the table.

Trent welcomed Joelle's interruption from his own thoughts as he got lifted her down from the chair and got her ready to go.

The hospital looked like a mad house when Trent and Joelle arrive. Making his way to the information desk, he asked the man sitting behind it where he could locate Shia. Flipping through his paperwork to locate her name, he switched to the computer.

"She's currently in surgery sir on the sixth floor."

"Thanks." Trent responded as he was issued a visitor's pass. That allowed him on the floor where they were working on his wife. Where all he could do was sit and wait. Two hours went by as Trent held a sleeping Joelle in his arms.

The doctor briskly approached the solemn man in the corner of the waiting room.

"Mr. Coleman?"

Trent looked up slowly, dread weighing heavy on his heart, and stood. "We have good news; we could successfully operate on your wife. She is in a coma due to severe head trauma. All of her vitals are good. The impact of the head on collision caused Shia to have a significant brain tissue injury. We're not sure how long she will be in a coma, but the surgery did go well so we are optimistic that she will pull through it. In the meantime it is good for the family to visit often and talk to her as much as possible." The doctor told him before retreating down the hall.

Trent closed his eyes to thank God as he sank back into the chair he had only just recently vacated. As the doctor left from the same direction, he had come.

"Oh no. Is there something I can do to help?" A familiar voice asked.

Trent felt moisture hit his fingers, and continued to let the tears flow not believing that his wife of two years was lying in a coma. His mind understood, but his heart was having a hard time catching up. If it ever did.

"No," he whispered to the woman without looking up. There was nothing this woman could do to help, unless she was in the miracle performing business. Otherwise, there was nothing.

"Yes there is. I'm concerned; I don't want you to go into shock."

Trent knew the woman was trying to be nice, but he wasn't in the mood. He finally looked up.

"Natalia?" He said recognizing the face, surprised to see her standing there.

"Yes and before you dismiss me because I feel as if that's what you're about to do. I can help you."

"How so?" Trent asked politely not caring either way.

"I heard what the doctor said to you." Natalia looked at him with sympathy in her eyes. I've seen what this can do to someone firsthand, with my father when my mother was in a similar situation. My father went into a massive depression and then died six months later. I wouldn't want that to happen to you. Let me help you."

Trent studied Natalia's gray eyes and could tell that she was genuinely concerned.

"Why do you care what happens to me? Thought you would hate me by now."

"I could never hate you Trent."

"I have to go." Trent told her, "I've got to check on Shia. See her for myself."

"Well take my number just in case." Natalia handed him a business card from her black exclusive collection Michael Kors bag. "I'm always available to listen."

Trent took the card without responding and watched Natalia walk away. He had needed a reason to get rid of Natalia. Seeing her here out the blue like this was strange to him and he was dealing with enough as it is. He'd phoned Leigh in the car on his way to the hospital and was waiting for her to arrive with the boys.

"How is she?" Leigh asked running up to Trent and embracing him with the boys in tow.

"She's in a coma. I was waiting for you before I went in to check on her."

"Okay." Leigh said taking Joelle and sitting in the waiting area with the boys while Trent went to check on Shia.

Walking into the intensive care unit Trent braced himself for what he would see. When he reached Shia's room, his heart almost broke in two when he saw the condition that her body was in. Shia's body was swaddled in a body cast. When he'd spoken to the nurse earlier she'd let him know that she had broken several bones in addition to her trauma and the air bag had broken her nose and blackened both of her eyes. She really was the worse for wear as far as Trent could see. However, to him in spite of all that she was beautiful to him. Watching her chest rise and fall with each breath made Trent feel as if God was bestowing personal blessings on him and his family. She was his world and nothing could happen to her.

Trent approached Shia's bed and stared down at his wife wishing that he could switch places with her. He knew she was a fighter through and one day soon she'd be home and they could laugh at how she was once bandaged like a monkey together.

Gently placing a kiss on her swollen cheek, he sat in the chair next to her bed and held her hand. Unable to keep the tears from releasing any longer he thanked God for sparing Shia's life.

**

Entering the house with a heavy heart and a sleeping Joelle in his arms, Trent felt the difference immediately. There wasn't a light on in the house, no food cooling in the kitchen, no wife to meet him at the door with a smile on her face, looking, and smelling like his eternal sunshine.

Glad that the twins were staying the night at Leigh's place. Trent put a sleeping Joelle to bed. Going into his and Shia's room sitting down on the bed Trent looked over at Shia's side and let the tears flow. He needed his wife. Lying back on the pillows she had placed so nicely, he grabbed hers and held it up to his face. Exhaling her scent, he clutched the pillow as if his life depended on it. He wouldn't wash the pillowcase until she came home. He needed to be able to smell her scent every day.

**

As the weeks began passing and Shia showed no signs of coming out of her coma, Trent realized he was going to need help at the house because it was beginning to look a wreck. He thought about calling Leigh and having her come over, but Trent knew that he ran her ragged. He still had Natalia's business card and even though they hadn't spoken in years, he knew that she would help him if need be, so he retrieved the business card and gave her a call.

"Hello." Natalia answered the phone, knowing that it was Trent on the other line. He didn't know that she had access to all of his phone lines.

"Hi." A soft male voice responded back.

"May I ask who this is?"

"This is Trent."

Natalia was elated when the caller identified himself.

"Trent?" she responded with a question in her voice not wanting him to know how happy she was to hear from him.

"Yes, I apologize for the intrusion; remember you gave me your business card at the hospital?"

"I remember." Natalia began as she sat down on the chaise in her family room. "How can I help you?"

"I may need a little help." Trent began sheepishly, not really knowing how to go about this conversation.

"Are you doing okay? How is your wife? You holding up okay?"

"As well as can be expected. I try not to think about it too much."

Natalia could hear the pain laced in his throat.

"What can I help you with?"

Trent was relieved when she asked him that question.

"My children, the house," he paused, "If you can think of it, then I need help with it."

"Of course I can help. Any time you need me. I can be available."

"How does now sound?" Trent said hopefully.

Natalia looked across the room at her silent visitors and smiled at them.

"Now is good. Text me your address and I will be on my way in about ten minutes."

"Thank you so much for this. You're saving my life."

"In more ways than one." Natalia replied hanging up the phone.

"Finally." Natalia addressed Phylicia, "I was beginning to think he wasn't going to call." Phylicia nodded her head in approval.

Natalia winked at her.

"Looks as if all systems are a go."

***

Trent surveyed the house and shook his head at the disarray surrounding him. Joelle was sitting in the middle of the floor playing with her Barbie's and she had their clothes, shoes, cars, accessories thrown all over the room.

Hearing the doorbell ring brightened Trent's mood. Natalia had arrived.

He opened the door and there she stood in her glamour. He couldn't deny that she was even more attractive than he remembered, but she was probably twice as crazy. Standing at his door at a petite 5.0' with a short, sassy haircut that displayed the delicate heart shape of her face he looked into her slightly slanted, bright gray eyes and fought off the old attraction he was feeling. His wife had only been in a coma for three weeks, but he was human, of course being around an attractive woman would make his body react, but he would respect his wife until the end.

"Thanks for showing up." Trent said opening the door wide so Natalia could enter.

"Of course. You need me, so here I AM. And not a moment too late I see."

Natalia said surveying the mess Trent's daughter had made in the living room. She hated cleaning of any capacity, which is why she had people clean her place, but she would have to play her part to be here, so clean she must. Now that she was finally invited in, it was time to put her plan to work.

Chapter 12

Leigh waited patiently at Trent's front door for him to let her in. Today was her day to pick up the children for Auntie Day and she was more excited than the kids were.

"Hello. How may we help you?" Natalia asked opening the door.

Leigh's face frowned up in confusion when a petite brown skin woman answered the door.

"Uh," Leigh paused, stepping back to look at the house number to make sure that she wasn't mistaken and in fact did have the right house, "Is Trent here?"

"He ran out." The woman smiled at Leigh, "You must be Leigh," she opened the door wide, "Come on in. The kids are expecting you."

Leigh entered the home cautiously and turned to face the woman. "I'm sorry; I didn't catch your name," she said eyeing the woman with an unfriendly expression on her face.

"I'm Natalia." The woman replied as she shut the door firmly behind Leigh. "I've been helping Trent out during this difficult time."

I bet you have. Leigh thought to herself as she took in how comfortable Natalia looked in her sister's house. "That's a nice robe you have on." Leigh was doing her best to keep her temper in check, but she knew that at any moment she was going to lose it.

Natalia looked down at the robe and then back up at Leigh with a smirk.

"Oh, I just threw this on because Joelle spilled something on my shirt."

Leigh narrowed her eyes when she saw Natalia's smirk. "I bought that for my sister. I would prefer it if you took it off and hung it back with the rest of her things."

Natalia's amused eyes collided with Leigh's angry ones, "Hey, no harm no foul," she laughed trying to lighten the mood. "I'll put it back."

"Thanks." Leigh snapped back with no traces of laughter present. "And please don't touch her things again."

Natalia flinched at Leigh's tone. "Or what?" She asked stepping into Leigh's personal space until their breaths began to do a tango dance as they synced in harmony.

Leigh opened her mouth to speak.

"Yo, I'm back!" Trent said as he entered the house and caught the two women in a face off with one another. "What's going on?" He asked in the awkward silence, "You two okay?"

"Who is this?" Leigh raised her voice to him without breaking eye contact with Natalia. "And why is she in my sister's house, in her robe?"

Trent knew how Leigh could be and was anticipating a full on battle.

"Natalia has helped me with the kids ever since Shia has been in the hospital."

"Yeah, I bet she's doing more than that. My sister has been in a coma for less than two months and you already have some woman all up in here in her space. That's really foul. I thought you loved Shia?"

"Make no doubts; Shia is the love of my life." Trent began to explain, "But while she's in her coma, I need help."

"I thought that's what I was here for?" Leigh asked looking him up and down and then looking at the attractive woman still clad in her sister's robe. "Look at her; she's so comfortable here she's wearing Shia's stuff! Trent it's disrespectful." Leigh was angry. She needed Shia to get out of her coma and sooner than later.

"Look, she's an old friend and she offered her help. Nothing is going on between us okay." Trent turned his focus on Natalia, "Please take off Shia's robe and don't touch her things. If I had been here when you went to get that robe, you wouldn't have that on. I can't have you in the house disrespecting my wife," he told her in a stern tone like he was talking to one of the children.

Natalia narrowed her eyes at Trent and left them in the hall, retreating to get her clothes.

Leigh shook her head at Natalia's retreating. "You know Shia would have a fit if she knew what was happening in her house. You need to get that woman out of here."

"Trust me; whatever you are thinking in your head is not really happening."

"I hear what you're telling me, but I'm telling you I'm a woman and I know something's. Like, that woman wants you. It's written all over her face.

"My loyalty is to my wife. Why do you care?"

"Because my sister is laid up in the hospital in a coma fighting for her life!" Leigh shrieked, "And you have some strange woman around her children. This is ludicrous." Leigh wished that she could shake some sense into Trent to make him see what was right before his eyes, but she held her tongue as Natalia reentered.

"Are the kids ready?" Leigh asked.

"Yes. I made sure they had a change of clothes and lunch for tomorrow." Natalia responded.

Leigh gave Natalia a '*whatever*' look as she helped the children out the door. When Natalia acted as if she was about to close the door Leigh almost had a fit.

"Oh no Ms. Thing. Grab your purse, you're leaving too."

Natalia looked at Leigh as if she'd lost her mind. "No, I'm a stay to help Trent get ready for work tomorrow."

"No ma'am, Trent is a grown man and knows how to get ready for work alone. Let's go."

Natalia narrowed her eyes at Leigh and realized she was going to be a problem and would need to be dealt with accordingly.

"Natalia, that is for the best." Trent said agreeing with Leigh, "I'm going to be on my way to the hospital to see Shia soon anyway."

Natalia nodded and said nothing as she grabbed her things and exited with Leigh and the children.

***

Natalia watched Leigh through malicious calculating eyes as she sat in the family room in the house. The two of them breathing the same air was like a time bomb waiting to ignite. Ever since their brief encounter the previous week, the two of them were like time bombs waiting to ignite.

Leigh continued playing with Joelle, choosing to ignore Natalia. She refused to acknowledge the woman who was trying rather successfully it seemed to take her sister's place.

"Lei are you cooking something for the kids or should I order some takeout for everyone?" Remi asked.

"You should ask the new Shia that question." Leigh replied rolling her eyes. "She seems to be campaigning to be wifey over there," she told Remi, grateful that her little sister had flown up from Florida the day before to help the family.

Remi quickly shifted her eyes between the two women. You could slice through the tension in the family room with a butcher knife. Remi watched as Natalia continued to clean up not paying any attention to Leigh's statements.

"Lei, Lei, what is wrong with you?" Remi chastised Leigh with her eyes, "She's only trying to help."

"No Remi that is what we are for. She is obviously trying to replace Shia. Remi please don't be so gullible."

A loud boom made both sisters glance in Natalia's direction as she slammed a plate down on the table.

"Do you have something you would like to say to me? I'm standing right here. Be a woman about yours and get it off your chest."

Disdain was apparent in Leigh's demeanor. "I have a lot to say actually." Leigh stood up and left Joelle playing on the floor coming to a stop directly in front of Natalia. Looking her up and down from head to toe.

"You think you're slick, trying to waltz in here and replace my sister, but I can see right through you. You're a fraud and I won't stop until I prove it. Why are you even here?"

"Listen sweetie, trust me when I tell you, you don't want to go toe to toe with a woman like me." Natalia moved in closer to Leigh until their noses were almost touching. "Now be a good little Auntie and play with the children, then carry your happy ass home," her eyes were flashing pure hatred as she stared Leigh down.

Remi quickly stepped in between the two women when she saw Leigh ball her hands into fists.

"This isn't your house, so if anyone is leaving it will be you." Leigh managed to spit out through clinched teeth.

'Trent and I are going to be together, so it will be my house soon enough, mark my words. That being said, I would like you to leave. You've overstayed your welcome." Natalia spat at her.

"Oh hell no!" Leigh shouted, startling Joelle who began to cry. Remi ran over to the teary toddler to comfort her as Leigh headed to Trent's office to confront him with a smug Natalia close on her heels.

Bursting into Trent's home office without bothering to knock Leigh was on a ten. Slamming the door behind her in Natalia's face and locking it, she went off on Trent.

"How dare you have this woman walking around this house trying to replace my sister? Shy is in a COMA, not dead! She's walking around talking about you and her are going to be together and this will be her house soon enough. You better start explaining and you better start right now before I begin to think that the two of you tried to kill my sister, so you could be together!" Leigh was clearly hysterical and didn't care.

Trent had glanced up when his office door had been thrown open and rose out of his chair slowly as Leigh ranted and raved in front of him.

"What do you two have going on Trent?" Leigh had tears falling freely from her eyes. "I thought you loved Shia." Leigh shook her head in disbelief, sadness radiating from every part of her body. "I thought you loved her…"

Trent walked around the office desk and reached for Leigh trying to pull her into a hug, but Leigh immediately moved just outside his reach. Trent dropped his arms.

"It's not what you think," he began to explain, "I really do need help with the kids and Natalia has been that. The kids like having her around and it makes my life that much easier."

Leigh shook her head in disbelief. "Remi and I have been here helping you as well. You don't need to do this. Something is up with that crazy chick. I can feel it. Get her out of here." Leigh raised pleading eyes up to his saddened ones, "Please don't do this. Shia would be rolling over in her hospital bed if she knew what was going on in this house."

"I have to do what's best for me and the kids right now. Shia would want me to do what needed to be done to ensure that they would be okay."

"You'll regret this." Leigh said as she began walking toward the office door to unlock it. "I promise you, you will." When she opened the door, Natalia was standing there with her ever-present smile in place.

"Hope you received all the information you needed. Now leave this house now please." Natalia said smugly.

Raising her hand Leigh smacked Natalia as hard as she could, removing the smile completely off her face. Leigh hadn't planned to hit her, but there was something about Natalia calling this her house that completely irked Leigh's nerves.

"I'm going to kill you!" Natalia shouted as she punched Leigh in her eye and continued her assault as Leigh grabbed her eye. Trent ran to separate the women immediately picking Natalia up off the floor to get her away from Leigh. Trent held on to a kicking and screaming Natalia allowing Leigh time to get herself together.

"You better watch your step. You're going to get yours. BELIEVE ME ON THAT!" Leigh spat at Natalia as she began to feel her eye swelling. "Trent, I can't believe that you're allowing this piece of trash in here, knowing how classy Shia is. Didn't anyone ever teach you that once you upgrade you never go back down?"

"What is going on in here?" Remi asked popping up from around the corner, seeing Trent holding an angry Natalia in his arms and observing Leigh holding her eye. No one answered Remi, they continued as if she wasn't there.

Natalia had finally calmed down in Trent's arms and turned to glare at Leigh. "You have some nerve," she told Leigh as she pushed her hair behind her ear. "You come in here and attack me and then call me a piece of trash." Natalia laughed long and hard, "The only trash present is you and we don't allow garbage in our rooms. I believe your place is outside. Now please exit my house. Obviously, you weren't taught any lessons on how to be a lady. If you knew how to take care of home instead of acting like a street urchin, maybe you would have a man. Now get out!"

Leigh narrowed her eyes on Natalia, as she addressed Trent. "As long as she's here," she pointed at Natalia, "I won't be coming back." Leigh quickly ran out the house and into her car leaving Remi behind.

Trent gingerly placed Natalia's feet back on the floor once he heard the front door slam.

"She's never allowed back in this house, is that understood?" Natalia told him.

"I can't agree to that and you know it. Leigh is Shia's sister and the children's aunt. They like and need to see her. It makes them feel close to their mom. So whatever it is you two have going on, you're going to need to fix it or you will have to leave."

"She attacked me and you're going to defend her just because she's the kid's aunt? That's really messed up of you."

"I'm not defending what she did, but we're all family and need to act like it. If you can't do that, then I may have to rethink your role in our life. You're only here to help, did you forget that?" Trent looked Natalia square in her eye, "You're going to have to get along with Leigh. If not, you're going to have to leave he repeated. I can't have my children's lives interrupted by foolishness from you. Whether you started it or not, is that understood?" Natalia stared at Trent in disbelief at his tone. "If you are still harboring any feelings about me and all this my house business, you need to leave it where it is. If you can't do that then with no questions asked you will have to go. Leigh may have been right. Having you here may be a very bad idea and a general lack of judgment on my part."

"You would let me go that easily? No fight or anything?"

Trent shook his head at her, "Natalia, we're not in a relationship. My family comes first. You know that already. Not you or anyone else will be the cause of their unhappiness. They're going through a lot right now and don't need any extra outside sources making their lives worse."

"I didn't mean to impose on family time. I can just go." Natalia huffed with an attitude.

"I still need help, the sisters can't be here forever, but if you feel that it's best for you to leave, then by all means, you can leave because if you stay you will have to get along with Leigh. I know she can be irritating, but her twin is in the hospital, so cut her some slack."

"That's fine, but she is going to have to keep her hands off me. I don't take kindly to people attacking me. I would hate for her to get hurt."

Natalia let that sentence hang in the air for a moment before leaving Trent to join the kids and Remi in the family room.

Trent followed behind her at a slower pace. He didn't know what to make of Natalia, but he knew that he couldn't allow her to disrupt his family life because god-willing Shia would be home eventually and wanted there to be peace when she returned.

"On second thought," Trent began entering the family room, "Maybe you should go. Family comes before everything." Trent walked back out not caring one way or the other if Natalia's feelings were hurt. He would be sure to get the locks changed in the morning.

***

Phylicia was growing impatient. She needed the heat to die down from her escape so that she could personally handle what needed to be done herself. First thing on her list was figuring out a way to handle Natalia.

She didn't appreciate how the tides were turning. Things were beginning to get out of hand and it was high time that she came out of retirement. Nothing seemed to be going the way she needed them to go. She hated sitting on the sideline waiting for results to ignite. Conducting her own research, she had discovered some very interesting information about Natalia. Like how she and Trent used to date. Phylicia had known she was right not to trust Natalia, but not for the reasons she had originally thought, turns out those reasons were trivial compared to finding out that Natalia was actually in love with Trent. That put things in a whole new prospective for Phylicia. Natalia had a whole other agenda, but what she didn't know was that she was up against the best and since she had sought out the best, Phylicia was going to give her exactly what she was looking for.

***

Remi had just put the children to bed when Leigh showed up at the house.

"I'm so glad that you are staying here for the time being. That Natalia woman had to go."

"I hate to say this, but she was doing a good job with the kids because they can be a handful. Joelle keeps asking about her."

"Joelle will get over it." Leigh replied. "Natalia is no good and she's up to something. She reminds me of crazy Phylicia. I don't know why exactly, but she does. Their personalities resemble."

"You know she broke out of that hospital she was in. Shia had called me to talk about that one night before she was in her accident."

"I know, I saw it on the news; same as Shy." Leigh snapped her fingers, "Matter of face, Shy was in the accident not too long after that. I wonder if Phylicia had something to do with it."

"Oh no." Remi began shaking her head, "Don't you go playing inch high private eye. You know what happened the last time you pulled a stunt like that." Leigh shuddered when she thought of the months that she had been kidnapped.

"Relax. I'm not going to do anything crazy. I just need to check on a few things to see what's what."

"I don't know Lei Lei. I have a bad feeling about this already. Let's let the police and detectives do their jobs. That's what they're paid to do." Remi suggested hesitantly.

"Of course you're right, but I need to know for me. Just so I can rest easy at night."

Remi continued shaking her head. She knew Leigh was going to do what she wanted, so arguing with her was futile.

"Well do what you feel is best."

Leigh smiled. "I sure will."

Chapter 13

"We need a new plan. Trent has let Shia's sister Remi move in."

"Why is that you think?" Phylicia asked Natalia patiently.

"I don't know. One day he's saying he wants me to stay and help, the next day he told me he didn't want a divided family and needed peace in his life for him and the children.

"So you were causing a disruption?"

Natalia didn't like the tone that Phylicia had taken.

"I wouldn't say that exactly."

"What would you say exactly? Were you coming on to Trent?"

"Of course not!" Natalia exclaimed quickly.

"You're not lying are you? You know, once someone lies to you; that trust can never be regained." Phylicia stared into Natalia's eyes unflinchingly.

"I know and I'm not lying."

"Okay, so why was the situation non peaceful?"

"Leigh didn't like me on sight. So she and I being in the same place will always a problem."

Phylicia said nothing. She knew better. Natalia had recruited her, thought up this brilliant plan to get Shia out the way, let Phylicia take the fall for it so that she could get Trent to herself. Phylicia loved the way that Natalia thought she could play her for a fool, but it would all come to a head, the game was about to begin changing.

Natalia watched Phylicia studying her in silence. She hoped that she was convincing enough with her answers. She didn't want Phylicia figuring her out. That would cause a whole new set of problems. Problems that Natalia herself had unleashed.

"Okay." Phylicia said nodding her head. She now knew what had to be done.

"Okay. What?" Natalia asked.

Phylicia only smiled. "Goodnight. Get some rest. We'll come up with a new plan in the morning." Natalia's eyes followed Phylicia's as she left the room.

Natalia didn't know what Phylicia's deal was, but she hoped that she didn't forget who had broken her out of that crappy hospital. Natalia had no problem calling the police letting them know where they could find her.

Phylicia was the queen of finding out information when she needed to and discovering everything about Natalia was at the top of her priority list. She and Natalia had known each other since Natalia was a teenager and while she may have been young at the time Phylicia hadn't been fooled. Natalia was one-step away from being a sociopath. She knew Natalia used to kill and torture animals as a small child, but wasn't sure if that behavior had continued in her teenage and young adult years. Phylicia had considered her in the category of a lessor sociopath. Meaning she had once believed her behavior wouldn't escalate into murder, but now she couldn't be quite too sure. With someone who had endured what Phylicia knew Natalia did as a teenager, she wasn't sure what she was capable of as an adult. Not that Phylicia thought she was better or worse than Natalia by any means. She just knew that she was not a sociopath. While she had done some things that regular people may deem evil and mean-spirited, Phylicia did have a heart and cared about others feelings. She wasn't born this way; she had been made this way. She had cared once upon a time, but after being married to a monster like her ex-husband Maxwell, she had almost given up on love anymore. Then, she'd met Trent and they had been magical together, that's why she couldn't let him go. No matter what happened in her life, she needed Trent by her side. Gazing at the photo Natalia had shown her of Trent and Shia; Phylicia had cut Shia's face out the photo and pasted the photo of her mug shot off the Internet onto the photo, so that now she and Trent's images stared back at her.

"I love you. We'll be together soon." Phylicia whispered to the photo. Laying the photo on the desk in the cave like room.

Cutting on the computer, Phylicia waited patiently as it booted up. Natalia was definitely playing with the wrong one. Phylicia thought. She lacked the intelligence to be in a league with the big guns and she was going to learn real soon being the object of Phylicia's wrath was a bad place to be.

Entering the code she had memorized when Natalia had used it once before, Phylicia opened the encrypted file she kept in the hidden folder on the computer. The file opened first showcasing a head shot of Natalia; then on the next page was the meat of what Phylicia was seeking; a full on twenty page background check on Natalia.

Reading each page with painstaking care, Phylicia made it a point to know as much information as possible about her enemies.

***

To hell with waiting for her to help me come up with a plan. Natalia thought to herself as she paced the top floor of the brownstone in that they were housed. She needed to think hard and fast. Every day that passed was one day less she had to make Trent see that her rightful place was with him and his children.

First, she had to find a way to get Phylicia out the picture faster. She's broken Phylicia out of the mental hospital to be the one to take the fall when Shia wound up dead, but ever since the initial breakout and emergency alert on the day she left the hospital, she'd heard nothing else about her escape on the news. Shia's head on collision hadn't made the news at all and Natalia was beginning to wonder if the police had been unable to piece the two incidents together. The truck had been impounded after the accident. Natalia had paid off a stranger to ram her head on and flee the scene, but now Natalia needed to find a way to link Phylicia to the accident so that the search for her could intensify. Natalia needed her out of her home immediately. She knew it was only a matter of time before she became a problem because Phylicia wasn't stupid by far and Natalia needed to remind herself to remember that.

Natalia glanced at the ceiling as she continued to pace. Picking up the phone, she dialed Trent's number.

"Hello?" Trent answered right away after seeing Natalia's name and number come on his cell screen.

"Hi." Natalia spoke softly into the receiver.

"What's up?" Trent asked after a beat passed and Natalia hadn't said anything, just breathing on the other end of his phone.

"Can I come and see you? It's important."

"You can't tell me over the phone?" Trent asked.

"It concerns information about Shia's accident. I think it would be better if we spoke in person."

"Okay. Get here as fast as you can."

"Be there in about fifteen." Natalia said hanging up the phone.

Phylicia hung up the receiver in the basement. Taking in what she heard.

***

Trent was anxious for Natalia to get there. He needed to hear what she knew about Shia's accident. The police didn't seem to have any leads and that was making Trent lose hope in the police system.

When Natalia finally arrived, she was like a volcano about to erupt and nothing was going to stop what she had to say.

"I think Phylicia had something to do with Shia's accident."

"What?" Trent eyed her suspiciously not even bothering to offer her a seat. "How would you know anything about Phylicia and who she is to me? I never mentioned her to you."

Natalia refused to focus on the fact that she was cold busted.

"Trent focus. Who didn't know about y'all's case it made the local news." Natalia stated matter-of-factly, "Anyway, I believe she had something to do with it."

"And why would you think that?" Trent asked her, waiting to hear what she would say.

"Umm," Natalia paused, "Just a feeling that I have. More like a hunch."

"A hunch huh?" Trent said continuing to eye her. "Did you take your hunch to the police?"

"Well, not exactly." Natalia paused, "I wanted to let you know first."

"And why is that? Afraid they'll ask how you know this information?" Trent asked her. He wasn't in the mood for Natalia's games today. If she had information on Shia that was one thing. If she was here to start some mess; that was another.

"Not at all." Natalia shot back, "I could always call in an anonymous tip."

Trent continued looking at her through narrowed eyes. Natalia wasn't making any kind of sense to him. If he didn't know any better, he would think that Natalia had something to do with Shia's accident.

"So, lemme ask you this, did you have anything to do with Shia's accident?"

Natalia looked him square in his eyes, "Of course not, why would I do something like that?" she asked him, "I don't even know your wife."

"Because I know what you used to be capable of." Trent said, "Even though you haven't shown any current signs of taking a simple old flame of love this far I have to ask because Shia hasn't done anything to anyone. She is an innocent bystander in all of this."

"Trent, listen to me," Natalia pleaded, I would never do anything to Shia. I'm looking forward to the day she comes home and I have an opportunity to meet her and let her know what wonderful children she has."

Trent only looked at her. He couldn't tell if she were sincere or not. In his heart, Trent honestly didn't think Natalia would intentionally hurt someone. He knew she could act drastic while in love, but he refused to think that that would extend to murder.

***

Phylicia listened on the headset as she observed Natalia speaking to Trent in his house. Smirking as she heard what Natalia was telling him, she could barely contain her amusement. Natalia was writing her own death certificate and didn't even know it. She must have forgotten that she had shown and told Phylicia all the ropes. Like having, the house taped. Making sure her head was covered Phylicia had heard enough, she began the journey back to the Brownstone to begin putting her plan in motion.

Back at the house, Phylicia put things into prospective very quickly. She knew that she wasn't going back to the hospital where they could hold her captive. They would have to kill her because she was never returning. Natalia had definitely done her background on Phylicia and knew that breaking Phylicia out of the hospital and pinning Shia's accident on her was a sure way to ensure they locked up Phylicia and threw away the key forever.

Natalia felt a chill in the air as soon as she walked through the door. Since a window had been left open in the living room Natalia took quick strides to go over and close it before she set her purse down.

Locking the window once she pulled it closed, she jerked her head to look over her shoulder. She had the eerie feeling that she was being watched. The house was library quiet so she would hear something if it moved, but nothing was moving.

Attempting to cut on the lamp that sat on an end table in the living room Natalia wasn't alarmed when it didn't turn on. *The bulb must have blown.* She thought to herself. Walking toward the light switch on the wall, she began to get alarmed when that light didn't come on either.

Reaching into the purse, she pulled out her razor blade and left her purse sitting on the sofa.

"Phylicia you psycho stop playing games. I know it's you. Stop hiding." Natalia yelled into the silence of the darkened house.

Phylicia watched Natalia from her crouched perch in the corner unmoving and smiled as she watched her twirling back and forth with her little razor blade in her hand for protection. Watching as she came closer and closer to the corner Phylicia was bidding her time. As soon as Natalia was standing right in front of her with her back to Phylicia, Phylicia stood slowly and put Natalia in a headlock while placing a handkerchief of chloroform over her nose as she struggled to get away flailing the blade around wildly. Phylicia kept the pressure on Natalia's neck until she felt her body begin to go limp.

***

Natalia woke in the basement a short time later chain linked to the wall. Mouth bound by a sock and tape she was unable to say or move any part of her body. She knew Phylicia had done this, but where was she?

"Hi sleepy head." Phylicia began in a singsong voice.

Natalia's eyes widened as Phylicia came into view and she saw what she was holding in her hands.

Phylicia smiled and it reminded Natalia of Jack Nicholson when he played the Joker in Batman. "You have been a very naughty girl." Phylicia continued, "And you will have to pay for your bad behavior."

Natalia began squirming on the wall trying her best to pull out of the chains, but there was no use, Phylicia had her locked in tight.

"What did you do you wonder?" Phylicia asked as she walked to the counter and placed the saw among the other tools laid out.

Looking up and staring her directly in Natalia's eyes, she appeared possessed.

"You attempted to take something from me that doesn't belong to you. Something that never belonged to you." Tears raced down Phylicia's face. "I would have been a perfect wife to him you know that?" Natalia shook her head as she saw the wild look Phylicia's face displayed.

"He never loved you Natalia. Why can't you get that through your head? You're chasing a man who never loved you and never will." Phylicia blinked rapidly trying to stop the tears. "He loves me, I know he married Shia, but he does love me at the end of the day. I was his first love and he will always love me."

Tears fell from Natalia's eyes as she listened to Phylicia. "You thought you would use me in your little scheme to get Shia out the way and have him to yourself, didn't you? ANSWER ME!" Phylicia yelled. Natalia frantically shook her head no.

"Yes you did and now you are trying to play me for stupid and I will not tolerate mockery." Phylicia spat at her. "You went to his house tonight to rat me out and only made yourself look guilty. Tsk, tsk, tsk." Phylicia wagged her finger back and forth, as she shook her head.

"Now why would you think something like that was a good idea sweetie?

Picking up a hand saw Phylicia's laugh made a screeching sound as she continued, "It always amazes me how the student wants to take over as the teacher without completing all of their lessons first. Shame on you." Phylicia said hitting the on switch on the saw.

Hearing the machinery purr to life Natalia yanked at the chains so hard she felt as if she had dislocated her shoulder.

"You are going to learn a valuable lesson today." Phylicia's voice suddenly turning cruel, cold, and evil. "You will learn to respect those that come before you."

Raising the saw, she brought it down and held it firmly as it ripped through Natalia's arm. Stopping just before it hit the bone Phylicia stepped back as Natalia struggled to scream behind the tape and sock stuffed in her mouth.

"Did that hurt honey?" She asked in a singsong voice again.

Bringing the saw down again Phylicia sliced another part of her arm almost to the bone. Natalia's muffled screams of agony bounced around the room.

"You should have never begun a game you weren't ready to play!" Phylicia screamed at her watching the blood ooze from Natalia's wounds onto the floor. Turning the saw off, she grabbed lemon juice and squirted it onto Natalia's arm. Natalia felt as if she would faint from the massive trauma and pain she was in. "What's wrong? Lemon juice will make you smell good."

Phylicia began laughing hysterically watching Natalia squirm even more as she pulled out the rubbing alcohol. "Now we must sterilize you, wouldn't want you to get infected now would we?" Pouring the alcohol over her opened wound, Phylicia watched as Natalia passed out, her body unable to bare another second of pain.

Natalia was startled back to consciousness by freezing ice-cold water being thrown on her.

"Wake up sunshine! No sleeping allowed." Natalia slumped her head. She noticed that Phylicia had bandaged her arm together.

Scooting up on the chair, Phylicia sat directly in front of Natalia. "Things are going to go a little differently now," she said leaning back in the chair placing her hands behind her head. "I do believe that now you are in a better state of mind to hear what I have to say."

Natalia eyed her warily, no fight left inside her. "We're going to play a new game now." Phylicia smiled suddenly displaying her pearly whites. "You're going to do as I say and you are going to like it, understand?"

Natalia continued looking at her, "Nod your head, so that I know you understand." Phylicia said smile vanishing when Natalia refused to cooperate. Picking up the hammer off the counter, "I would hate for you to lose the use of your fingers because you're going to need them;" she eyed Natalia inquiry.

Natalia began nodding uncontrollably. "So glad we're in agreement." Phylicia said smiling again.

"You're going to get back on Trent's good side because you have to lead him to me. However, don't worry, you're thinking days are over and done. From now on, I'll do all the thinking and you'll do all the bidding. Kay." Phylicia said sweetly.

"Before you say why you would do something like that and blah, blah, blah let me explain. I know all about your little incident with your old roommate Erikka. Natalia's eyes widened and then narrowed.

"Yup," Phylicia emphasized popping her lips, "Know all about it. See, I do research too. Amazing how secrets tend to not be so secret." Phylicia threw numerous emails from Natalia's account that were supposedly sent by Erikka. Tyrique must be a great friend huh? Where'd you meet him?" Phylicia stared at Natalia's eyes trying to sear her soul watching as she tried to say something, but couldn't because her mouth was taped. "I always admired students that got into NYU; they are so incredibly intelligent considering how hard it is to get into that school. However, it's interesting just how intelligent people can be. Natalia, you are pretty intelligent, but meeting up with Tyrique makes you almost genius. How cool is it to have a friend that not only specializes in graphic design, thus being able to create authentic postcards, but can also forge postage from all over the world." Phylicia nodded her head in admiration, "Now that is pretty impressive. What gets me though is how two very intelligent individuals don't know that email can be hacked, and send emails discussing everything they were doing and the plans they come up with." Phylicia shook her head, "I mean who does that?" She laughed hysterically staring at Natalia. "Damn shame what happened to Erikka, a paper weight though, really?" Phylicia mocked. "Must have been your first time." Phylicia continued laughing.

Reaching up Phylicia pulled the tape off Natalia's mouth and pulled out the sock.

"You're crazy," were the first words Natalia uttered from her lips.

165

"Say what you will, but one false move from you and that little Erikka incident will be public knowledge in a matter of minutes and then your freedom will be taken from you." Phylicia snapped her fingers, "Just like that. Trust me, I know."

Phylicia had painted Natalia into a corner. Losing her freedom was not an option, there was unfinished business that Natalia had to attend to, and she refused to have that taken from her. She hated that she had lost the advantage and Phylicia was now in charge. "What do I have to do?" Natalia asked, resigned in a flat tone.

"Well for starters a little enthusiasm would be nice." Phylicia smiled at her.

Natalia flashed her a fake smile and sat waiting for Phylicia's next move. She wanted to kill Phylicia and the two of them would definitely have their day. Natalia was going to make sure of it. Sooner or later Phylicia was going to slip up and make a mistake and Natalia wanted to make sure she was there, so that when Phylicia fell, there would be no return.

Chapter 14

Listening to the monitors beeping in Shia's hospital room, Trent watched her chest rise and fall with each breath she took. He needed Shia to pull through more than anything in the world.

"Baby, I love you," he began speaking softly into her ear leaning over from the chair he was sitting next to her bed.

"I need you to pull through this for me and our family. The kids need you." Trent just wanted to keep talking to her. The doctors told him that talking to her every day was good; that she could hear him.

"Please pull through this, your man needs you." Trent grabbed her hand, brought it to his lips to kiss it, and then placed it over his heart.

"Can you feel that baby? My heart beats in sync with yours. If yours stops, so will mine. I need you," he laid his head on the pillow next to hers.

One of the nurses entered the room to check Shia's vitals.

"How are you doing today? The nurse asked him.

Trent kept his face next to Shia's. "I'm okay."

"If you want to stay overnight, I can bring you a pillow." The nurse offered him.

"No thank you." Trent swallowed audibly. "I have to get home to the kids, but I'll be back first thing in the morning."

"Ok hun. Get some rest." The nurse told him.

Trent rose out the chair and went to the door, then turned back to face the nurse, "Do you think she knows I visit her?" Trent asked the nurse trying to keep the tears from falling.

"Of course she does sweetie. Always." The nurse said walking up to him and giving him a hug seeing the tears threatening to fall from his eyes.

"Good. I hope my voice keeps her holding on. She's all I have."

The nurse let him go. "She knows." The nurse told him sympathetically. "She'll pull through this. Just keep loving her like you have been and God will take care of the rest."

Trent was grateful for the nurse's kind words as he exited the hospital. He'd needed to hear them so that he could have peace of mind.

When Trent returned home, he was surprised to see every light in the house cut on. Trent hurried and parked his truck so that he could run inside.

"What's going on?" He shouted through the house. "Remi! Where are you?" Remi ran into the foyer with a frantic Leigh right behind her.

Seeing Leigh made Trent want to panic, but he fought to keep his composure. "What is going on?" He asked again, more calmly.

"Joelle is hiding somewhere." Remi responded.

"Is that all?" Trent instantly relaxed, "You two almost made me lose my mind. How long has she been hiding?"

"Two hours." Remi cringed.

Trent wasn't in the mood for this right now. He needed peace. He prayed his wife came out of her coma soon.

"Joelle, that's enough playtime. Come out right now." Trent yelled in a stern tone expecting Joelle to pop up out of wherever she was hiding.

"Trent we've tried that and checked everywhere. She's not here."

"What do you mean not here?" Trent turned angry eyes on her, "If she's not here, where else would she be?" Redirecting his wrath to Remi, "I leave my daughter in your care for a couple of hours and you lose her. Where could she have gone?"

"We're sorry. We don't know where she is."

Trent went to his bedroom and checked under the bed. He had to find his baby girl. She was all he had of him and Shia. He couldn't live with himself if something happened to Joelle.

He tried to think like a toddler to figure out where she had wondered too, when the doorbell rang.

Trent raced to the front door, throwing it open.

There stood Natalia with a sleeping Joelle cradled in her arms. Trent closed his eyes in relief. His baby girl had been found.

Graciously taking Joelle out of Natalia's arms Trent didn't know whether to hug her or call the police for kidnapping.

"I was coming over to talk to you about the other night and saw this little one lying in the grass fast asleep."

"Thanks for being here Natalia. I don't know how she got out the house."

"Me either." Leigh said accusingly staring at Natalia through suspicious eyes. "Seems a little convenient to me. Don't you think so Remi?"

"Yeah, crazy how Joelle suddenly disappears and out of nowhere reappears with Natalia who shows up out of nowhere unannounced. Seems very convenient to me as well, especially since we searched high and low for her." Remi said eyeing Natalia as well.

"Doesn't matter." Trent said breaking the tension, "I'm just glad Joelle is back safely. " Come on in Natalia. You said you wanted to talk."

Trent led Natalia to the family room and sat on the chaise lying Joelle across his lap as to not disturb her sleep.

"What's up?" Trent asked.

Natalia shrugged, "I want to apologize about the other day. I was very inappropriate and out of line. Please forgive me."

"You found my little girl. I'd forgive you anything."

Natalia gazed at him in appreciation.

Remi and Leigh observed Trent and Natalia's interaction from the hallway.

"I don't trust this heifer. Something is up with her." Leigh whispered to Remi.

"I know you don't, but I don't know what we can do about the situation. I can't stay here forever. I have to get back to Florida in a couple of days.

Leigh understood that Remi had to get back to her life; she'd already been up here with them for weeks hoping that Shia would wake out of her coma.

Leigh sighed, "I know you have to leave soon. We are just going to have to figure something out."

***

Remi thought Shia looked so peaceful lying in her hospital bed. It almost appeared as if she were merely asleep and not in a coma.

"She doesn't even look as if she's been in an accident anymore."

171

"I know." Leigh replied to Remi's statement. The nurses had removed all of Shia's casts. The only thing left was her head wrap and the nurses had said that would be coming off soon. "She looks good. Almost brand new."

"I miss her."

"I know you do, but Shia will fight through and be stronger than ever. " You'll see." Leigh reassured Remi.

"I'll take your word for it." Remi replied leaning down to kiss Shia on the forehead. "I love you Shy, get better okay. We want you to pull out of this so that you can come on home." Remi whispered hovering over her.

It broke Leigh's heart, watching the exchange. She wondered how many bad things could happen to one family. It was as if they were the cursed sisters from Maryland. Their parents had been murdered then sat on fire, she and Remi had been kidnapped, Shia's wedding had literally gone up in flames, Trent had almost died, and now this, Shia gets in a car accident that was so bad she was stuck in a coma fighting for her life. Leigh buried her face in her hands. She wondered if anyone had ever thought about adding a reset button to life because if there was ever a time she wanted to press it. The time was now.

***

"I'm back in." Natalia told Phylicia when she hung up the phone with Trent. It was a couple of days after the incident of Joelle going missing.

"Perfect. I knew that little incident with his daughter would make him trust you again." Phylicia was giddy with excitement. Her plan had worked. She'd had broken into the house one day when she knew it would be empty and stolen one of the spare keys to the back door. She'd had Natalia go take a sleeping Joelle out the house and make it seem as if she were kidnapped. Then, she had Natalia reappear with Joelle in her arms to make her look like the hero. With Remi heading back home, Trent now trusted Natalia enough to invite her back into his home to help him with the children.

Natalia turned away from Phylicia and her look of glee angry with herself. This whole situation was her fault. She never should have concocted a plan to have Phylicia broken out of the hospital. Her little plan had backfired and now she was nothing more than a pawn in a game that she had created, but didn't know the rules of how to play.

"Penny for your thoughts?" Phylicia asked Natalia.

"I have nothing to say to you." Natalia retorted in a nasty tone.

Phylicia stood up suddenly getting directly in Natalia's face.

"Careful," she grasped Natalia's heavily bandaged arm and applied pressure instantly making tears spring to Natalia's eyes from the pain, "I would hate to see something happen to your other arm."

Natalia tried to pull her arm away, but Phylicia refused to let it go gripping it harder until blood began to seep through the bandage to the surface.

"I know you're angry, but I would advise you to accept your current situation." Phylicia pulled Natalia in close and kissed her forehead. "Don't make me have to kill you," she whispered into her hair as she hugged her. "You're in tracing. Accept this gift. I'm giving you."

Natalia turned teary pain filled eyes on Phylicia.

"And I'm curious as to what gift that would be?"

Phylicia beamed a smile at her. "Life. Now get you some sleep it's going to be a long couple of days.

***

Leigh was in a funky mood. She had just left Remi at JFK airport and was pulling up at Trent's house right in time to see Natalia enter the house.

For the life of Leigh, she couldn't understand why Trent insisted on having this girl around.

Why is she here?" Leigh asked as soon as she entered the house. Trent sighed. He was tired of Leigh's attitude.

"Leigh, can we not do this today? I'm exhausted. I just got back from seeing Shy and really came home to relax."

Leigh saw the tired lines etched on Trent's face and lay off him a little.

"Ok, go lie down and get some rest. I'll take care of things here."

Trent gave her a grateful smile as he retreated to his and Shia's bedroom.

As soon as Trent left the room, Leigh attacked Natalia like a vulture.

"Why do you keep coming back here? Your services are not needed."

"Trent seems to think otherwise." Natalia told her without looking up as she dusted the furniture in the living room.

Leigh grabbed Natalia by her arm. Natalia screamed out in pain and dropped the duster to hold her arm. Leigh jumped back shocked by Natalia's reaction.

"Don't touch me!" Natalia cried out as she continued holding on to her arm.

"Are you okay?" Leigh asked shortly forgetting her beef with Natalia and genuinely concerned.

"Leave me alone. If you hadn't touched me. This wouldn't even be a problem." Natalia snidely remarked. Leigh's moment of concern was over and done.

"If you weren't here there wouldn't be any problems." An agitated Leigh pointed out.

"Okay, let me say this and I'm only going to say it once, so listen very carefully. I am here as long as Trent wants me here. I'm not going anywhere. Do you understand? I am not going anywhere," Natalia repeated slowly, "Until he tells me himself that he no longer wants me here." Natalia took one-step toward Leigh, "I really don't want to hurt you, but you keep forcing my hand, then I'm no longer responsible for anything that happens after that."

"Please Natalia!" Leigh responded in a nasty tone. "No one is afraid of you."

"That's almost funny because you should be." Natalia retrieved her duster off the floor and exited the room leaving her statement lingering in the air.

Natalia had to stop allowing Leigh to unnerve her because she was going to end up doing her bodily harm and that wasn't part of the plan. Tapping on Trent's bedroom door lightly, Natalia pushed open the door to witness him lying in the bed curled up under the cover with a photo of Shia laying on his chest.

Natalia thought he looked adorable. Disrobing, she joined him in the plush bed curled up next to him. Feeling the warm body behind him, Trent instantly turned to draw her in close. He missed his wife. Falling deeper into his dream, he imagined them to be in Cancun for a little get away from their everyday lives and the children.

When she began kissing him on his neck Trent began submitting to her touch, he always enjoyed making love to his wife. When she got on top of him and began to ride him Trent smiled in his sleep. Shia knew how much he enjoyed when she rode him like that. She knew exactly how he liked it fast and steady and when he came, she came with him. He was in heaven.

Trent's eyes popped open suddenly. His dream had felt too good and so real. Turning his head, he saw Natalia lying next to him grinning.

"What the...?" Trent jumped up from the bed.

"What are you doing in my room?" Taking in her nude body. Trent began shaking his head, "What just happened?"

"You just sexed me up real good." Natalia paused for dramatic effect, "And you liked it."

"I thought you were my wife I was asleep."

"Prove it." Natalia stated smugly.

"I never would have touched you had I been fully awake."

"No judge and jury would believe you."

"Trent, Joelle is asking for her daddy." Leigh said carrying a pouting Joelle in her arms into Trent's room.

Leigh stopped short taking in the scene in front of her. Trent standing by the bed naked with an angry scrawl on his face and Natalia laying in the bed also naked as if she belonged there.

Putting Joelle down in the hall, Leigh closed and locked the door behind her.

"Leigh it's not what you think." Trent began explaining as he reached down and put his boxers on.

Leigh wasn't listening to him; she raced to the bed and began throwing blows at Natalia. Turning her face into her personal punching bag. She wanted her face dripping with blood and she wasn't going to stop until that happened.

Remembering Natalia's battered arm Leigh started in on that. She wasn't going to be satisfied until she beat Natalia half to death. Natalia screamed out in pain when Leigh began attacking her arm.

Trent didn't want to, but was forced to break up the fight. Pulling Leigh off of Natalia, he didn't feel sorry Natalia at all. He could see the blood oozing from her arm.

"So on top of trying to get at my sister's man; you're messing up her sheets you psycho bitch! Get out of my sister's house right now and if you come back I promise you you'll regret it for the rest of your life." Leigh yelled from midair still being held up and away from Natalia by Trent.

Natalia rose out the bed slowly keeping her arm elevated. She was in excruciating pain, but refused to show them another weak moment. Hastily putting her clothes on her retreated from the room.

"Do not let her back in this house for any reason. She is the devil in the flesh."

Leigh yelled at Trent as she stepped back up in the hall to pick a screaming Joelle up off the floor.

"Shia would not stand for all of this foolishness in her house and you need to burn that damn bed."

"I know Shia wouldn't approve of what has been happening all I've been trying to do is what's best for the kids."

"Well, no more outside sources." Leigh gave him a pointed look. "We are a family unit and have to protect one another. Since Shia has been in her coma, everything has been going downhill. I will not tell my sister about this when she does come home and contrary to what everyone else seems to think, *my* sister *will* be coming home!"

Trent took a sniffling Joelle out of Leigh's arms and sat on the bed.

"I miss my wife," he said kissing Joelle on the forehead. "I'm not used to doing all of this house and kid stuff alone."

Leigh knelt in front of him refusing to touch the bed Natalia had recently vacated.

"That's why Remi came and I'm here now. We all miss Shy; so we have to band together so that we can get through this situation together leaning on one another."

Leigh stared into his. "Okay. We sisters are thick as thieves and we have each other's backs, as well as yours since you're our sister's husband. Don't forget that."

Trent pulled her in for a hug. "I won't."

***

Phylicia removed the binoculars from her face; shaking her head at the debacle, she had just witnessed. *Therefore, Natalia wanted to play hardball.* She thought to herself. She had completely underestimated Natalia, she thought that little stunt she pulled was going to ruin what Phylicia had planned, but in time, they would all see nothing could stop the inevitable.

***

Natalia opened the door to her house and stopped short when she saw Phylicia sitting on the stairs that led to the upstairs part of the house with a welcoming smile on her face and a whip in her hand.

"Why are you waiting for me?"

"Because you are having a hard time following directions and like you have to do with bad children, you must be punished."

"What did I do to not follow directions?"

"You know what you did. No time for talking. Strip." Phylicia told her standing up on the stairs to begin walking toward her.

Natalia eyed her as if she was stupid. "You're crazy. I'm not striping anything." Phylicia swung the whip and it connected with the arm Natalia had bandaged forcing her to scream out in pain.

"Oh, but you are." Phylicia swung the whip again forcing it to snake around Natalia's ankle and then she pulled it hard causing Natalia to topple over onto the floor.

"Strip." Phylicia demanded now standing over top of Natalia with the whip raised above her head. "Don't you know the sooner you learn to do what you're told the less pain you will have to endure?"

Natalia felt as if her body was on fire from where the whip had struck her. Trying to calm her raging emotions she was going to make it a point to see that Phylicia got what was coming to her.

Swinging the whip down on her back Phylicia needed Natalia to understand that she meant business. Natalia withered in pain from the contact of the whip. Phylicia's eyes began flashing, "You strip right now, or I will kill you on this floor." Phylicia was fed up and done with the games.

Battered beyond anything that she knew, Natalia slowly began to remove the clothes from her body. She wasn't the scared type of girl, but having her arm cut down to the white meat was traumatic for her. She wasn't in Phylicia's league at all.

"Good girl." Phylicia said kneeling down by her head so she could speak directly into Natalia's ear, "If you learn to submit faster, then we won't have any problems." Once Natalia had all her clothes off, Phylicia had her stand in the middle of the floor in the room and proceeded to swing the whip until her whole body was covered in welts.

"Now, will you be a good girl?" Phylicia continued without waiting for an answer. "I saw you rape Trent and before you deny that it was rape," Phylicia held up her hand when she saw that Natalia was about to begin to protest, "I saw the whole thing with my own two eyes."

As she kept swinging the whip Phylicia continued to speak, "It's rather sad actually what you have resorted to."

"Me?" Natalia spat out refusing to be quiet any longer, despite the punishment that she was enduring. "And you think you're so much better than me right?"

"Shut up!" Phylicia shouted bringing the whip down across Natalia's mouth splitting her lip open. Phylicia smiled when she saw the first drop of blood begin to drizzle down Natalia's face.

"Your pain makes me happy, you know that?"

"Psycho bitch!" Natalia spat blood at her with tears running down her face. She was beginning to fear Phylicia and she knew Phylicia knew it and was enjoying it. However, even with all that being said she had to let her know how she felt.

"You're the one that misbehaves and you call me the psycho one? I find that absolutely laughable." Phylicia told her, bringing the whip down even harder.

"What do you want from me?" Natalia cried.

"To play a game."

"I'm not into games."

"Now Natalia, that is not true." Phylicia shook her finger disapprovingly. "You're the one that began this game of hunter and prey. You turned me into a prey, while you hunted me," Phylicia clapped her hands together in glee, "but my game is so much better than that." Phylicia stopped swinging the whip and stood nose to nose with Natalia, "Let me introduce myself," she held out her hand for Natalia to shake, but her arm was in such bad shape Phylicia had to lift it for her, "I'm the Puppetmaster and you my dear are the puppet." Leaning closer in so their noses did touch Phylicia whispered, "And I am going to enjoy making you dance."

***

Natalia was covered up from head to toe. Her body had more bruises than the world could handle seeing. Pulling her hat down further over her head she walked through the building quickly. She was on a mission and she had to operate very fast.

After taking the stairs two at a time, she had finally made it to the floor that she was seeking. Easing out the staircase slowly glad to see no one lingering in the hall, she made a beeline for the room she was seeking. Certifying that she wouldn't be interrupted, she sashayed in and shut the door behind her.

Walking toward the bed she gazed down at Shia still confined in her coma world and picked up one of the pillows that were lying in a chair next to the bed. Holding the pillow over Shia's face, she gently pressed the pillow down on her face and waited patiently for her heart monitor to flat line.

Natalia jumped a little when a tap came at the door. Lifting the pillow she quickly through it in the chair and bowed her head, closing her eyes.

"Amen," she said a few seconds later as she watched the nurse check Shia's vitals.

"Hello Ms. Are you a family member?"

"Yes." Natalia responded without hesitating.

"Ok, I don't see a visitor pass on you though, dear. You will need to get one of those downstairs at the information desk if you want to visit with her any longer. Otherwise, you will have to leave." The nurse told her politely, but firmly.

"Thank you." Natalia mumbled as she exited the room, her mission incomplete. She would have to double back later in the week to finish the job that she had been assigned to do.

Chapter 15

L eigh was back on her investigation game. She was in
search of cold facts and she needed answers immediately.
She had a good inkling that Phylicia was somehow involved in
Shia's accident.

Pulling into the parking lot of Kirby Forensic Psychiatric
Center on Wards Island, where Phylicia had escaped from,
Leigh was seeking answers.

"Hello Ms. How may we help you?

"Hi." Leigh said to the receptionist, "I'm here to get some information on a Phylicia Taylor. She recently escaped an-"

"Oh no." The receptionist spoke in a hurried tone, "We can't give out information on patients here. Past or present."

"Is there a supervisor or someone that I can speak with that will give me answers?"

"No ma'am. There is no one that can divulge that information to you. Have a nice day.

Leigh felt as if the receptionist was rushing her back out the door as quickly as possible.

Retreating from the building, Leigh found herself back in the parking lot where she started without a lead. With no other leads at the moment and the day off from work, she first hit up her friend Shay to see what was popping off.

Shay answered on the first ring, "What's up, Chica?"

"Hey Shay." Leigh mumbled in a flat tone

"Honey you got to pull that tone together. That is not hot. Imagine if I were your man, I wouldn't want to do you, with you sounding like that. And you called me, not vice versa, so how I answer and you sound like you mad?"

Leigh laughed in spite of herself. Shay was a trip. "I just didn't break no ground with this Shia thing."

"Oh, I'm sorry. Give it time. It will piece itself together."

"Yeah, I guess so."

"Don't sound so down. What are you about to do now?"

"I haven't decided yet."

"Oh okay." Shay's breathing suddenly changed and got breathless.

"Shay what are you doing? Getting it in with me on the phone?" Leigh was disgusted.

"Sorry, you called and I answered, but I gotta go." Shay hung up in her ear.

Leigh shook her head as she put her cell back in her purse. She needed some new friends she thought. With nowhere else to go, Leigh decided to stop back by her house to see what Ty had going on. Since he could work from home because he was a freelancer she let him stay over at her place the previous night instead of truck it back home to the Bronx.

Walking into her apartment, Leigh heard moaning coming out of her living room causing her to halt immediately.

"What in the hell?" she thought. Tiptoeing towards the sound, she was shocked and disgusted by the scene that played out before her eyes.

Tyrique's eyes were closed as he mumbled, "Oh shit." Shay was slobbing the hell out his dick. Grabbing the back of her head with both hands, he helped her deep throat his meat. She was taking in every inch like a pro. He had never had nothing that felt like this before. The women he usually messed with didn't know what they were doing including Leigh. Shay could give Superhead a run for her money.

"Damn boo, you taste so good. I could lick you all night."

"Baby, you can lick my shit whenever you want to. I need all the porno head I can get."

"What is going on in here?"

Tyrique's whole body froze, as Shay abruptly stopped sucking, gasping as she tried to hide behind him.

Moving his hands to cover his meat, Tyrique groaned inwardly as he slowly opened his eyes, looking into Leigh's disapproving eyes, he knew some shit was about to go down.

Using one arm to protect her face, as Leigh began approaching her where she hid behind the chair, Shay began explaining, "Shay, I know how this looks."

"Bitch, are you crazy?" Leigh screamed, punching Shay in the face. "What the hell you doing in here sucking my man's dick in my house?"

Shay tried to block the blows as Leigh started going in on her body.

"STOP!" Tyrique yelled as he grabbed Leigh by the waist, picking her up off of Shay, he knew how far that Leigh could take it; she didn't play and go for all the bullshit.

"Tyrique put me down. I'm a fuck this bitch up."

"No you not, calm down."

Turning angry eyes on him, "What the hell you doing allowing Shay to suck dick in my house?" Leigh began swinging on him.

"Leigh, it's not what you think."

"Bitch, was I talking to you?" Leigh said, kicking her legs out to try and kick Shay while Tyrique carried her further away, "I'm gonna fuck you up so good, you gonna wish you had never met me. Dumb ass hoe. Wait until I get free."

Shay's eyes widened in disbelief. Leigh smirked at her, "Did you think I was just gonna let this shit slide? If you did, you a dumb hoe."

"Leigh, let me explain."

"Ain't nothing to explain, but this ass whipping I'm about to deliver." Leigh said struggling against Tyrique trying to get free.

"Leigh, will you calm down so Shay can get dressed?" Tyrique asked. Trying to hold on to her until he could get Shay safely out the apartment.

"No, that hoe can stay right there, with her simple ass." " Yo, get up and put your clothes on." Tyrique commanded Shay.

Leigh could hear Shay crying, looking down she saw her face streaked with tears and blood shot red eyes.

"Shut up." Leigh said in disgust still fighting Tyrique.

"Yo, you gonna have to chill." Tyrique told Leigh tightening his grip on her.

"To hell with you and her. I'm about to take care of this right now."

Glaring down at Shay from Tyrique's arms, "Get out my house." Leigh screamed, "Before I kill you!"

"Aye let her get dressed. She bout to roll." Tyrique said though Shay had yet to move.

"Hell no, she's not getting dressed in my house." Glaring at Shay again, "Bitch if I repeat myself and don't see movement, I swear I will split your shit."

Shay was humiliated beyond reason. Slowly moving toward the door so as not to further aggravate Leigh, she left without putting her clothes on, looking back or saying a word.

"And you can get your stuff and get out!" Leigh shouted once Shay was gone and Tyrique put her down. "She grabbed up his clothes and threw them into the hallway.

"I know you better stop throwing my stuff out in the hallway, what is wrong with you?"

"I'm not dealing with this. You will not and I repeat will not cheat on me. How about that! Now get stuff and get out."

"What are you talking about?"

"Tyrique, don't stand there and play dumb with me. You know exactly what I'm talking about. You make me sick! I give you everything all of me and you have my own friend in here, in my house giving you a head job disrespecting where I lay my head at night."

"I can explain if you let me." Tyrique kept the calm cool voice.

"Explain what?" Leigh was a long way past the point of explanations, stopping to look at him in the midst of throwing his things out the door. "Explain how you and Shay felt like it was okay to be in my house carrying on with this foolishness?" Leigh crossed her arms. "I really do want to see you try to explain yourself out of this one."

"Just listen for a minute…"

"Listen to what? Don't play yourself and try to tell me that what I saw with my own eyes wasn't what was happening

189

because I know for a fact that it was. I'm neither blind nor stupid. Whom do you think that you're fooling? I'm done with you and your lying and cheating ways. Get out my house."

"Aight fine, don't even listen to what I have to say." Leigh couldn't believe that he was actually trying to be the one with an attitude.

"I know you don't have an attitude. You're seriously embarrassing yourself. I don't need this crap in my life. I'm better off without you."

"So, you don't think that you have any fault in this situation at all?"

Leigh stood erect for a moment and then walked over to him very slowly, "What is my fault exactly? The fact that I came home early and you got caught? You nigga you busted. Just admit it and keep it moving."

"You need to chill out. I'm not going anywhere. I have an online Madden tournament in a few minutes and I ain't gonna miss it because you over here trippin'."

"You try to play Madden on my damn TV and we are going to have a serious misunderstanding. You have ten minutes to remove yourself." Leigh said before going into her bedroom and shutting the door.

***

Coming out of her room Leigh saw Tyrique sitting on her sofa playing Madden in the den as if it was a regular evening, made

Leigh went to take a frying pan and smash it into the side of his head. Smacking the controller out his hand Leigh was looking for a fight.

"Have you lost your damn mind? Think you gonna be in my damn house playing video games like you ain't have Shay up in here sucking your dick, with your dumb ass."

Tyrique stared at the controller on the floor and counted to ten before he completely lost his cool and broke Leigh's face with his fist. "She was here, you weren't. I did what I had to do." Tyrique smirked. Waiting to see what she would do with that information.

Leigh slapped Tyrique across his face so hard that his saliva hit the wall.

"This is not a joking matter. Shay's not just some random chick, she was my friend."

Tyrique snorted, "She was never your friend. Just like I was never your man."

"What!" Leigh shouted. "What are you playing some kind of game? You can't just be messing with people's lives like this. It will get you killed."

"Who's gonna kill me? You?" Tyrique looked up at her. "You came hollarin' at me. I didn't approach you. You called yourself my man. I never said that. Now you sitting here telling me that you were never my man?" Leigh sat there mad, hurt, and confused. She had found another Kodi after all.

"Everything ain't always what you think it is." Tyrique grabbed his jacket off the chair and turned toward the door getting ready to leave Leigh's apartment.

"You forgot something."

"What?" Tyrique said with an attitude as he turned back around and his face encountered his PlayStation knocking him out cold.

Leigh laughed as Tyrique's body hit the floor. Dropping and breaking the PlayStation by his body Leigh opened her front door. Walking back over to Tyrique's unconscious body Leigh smiled, now she felt vindicated. Grabbing each of his ankles in her hands, she dragged his body out her front door and down the hallway. Removing his cell phone from his hip, she went back into her apartment and picked up the broken PlayStation. Returning to the hall, she laid the PlayStation on top of his chest then strolled back in her apartment and bolted the door.

Having a seat in her love seat, Leigh took her time going through Tyrique's cell phone. She discovered that he had a ton of messages from Shay, which was very surprising to her because even though Shay had been there the day they met at the train station; they had never had another encounter with one another Leigh thought.

Scrolling through the messages, she was amazed that he'd kept all these messages in his phone. Trying to find the very first message Leigh was amazed to see messages between Shay and Tyrique dated before he had randomly introduced himself to her at the train station. As Leigh went through the messages, she began to notice that the meeting hadn't been so random after all.

198 days ago 8:50PM, Mar 13
I luv u baby

198 days ago 8:59PM, Mar 13
You should

198 days ago 10:00PM, Mar 13
Everything is set for tomorrow. I convinced her to take the train. She's usually on the bourgie side, but she said yeah. So plz b there n time.

198 days ago 10:35PM, Mar 13
Aight bet. I'll b there.

197 days ago 12:15PM, Mar 14
We're waiting for the E. Where r u?

197 days ago 12:45PM, Mar 14
Already here 2 ur right peep the hat u just bought me

197 days ago 12:45, Mar 14

Ur looking mighty sexy over there. Can't wait to get u home.

197 days ago 12:48PM, Mar 14
U gonna have the whipped cream and honey ready?

197 days ago 12:48PM, Mar 14
U already know how we do....i'm a have a whole lot more than that ready

197 days ago 12:49PM, Mar 14
Bet. I'm about 2 approach her. Love u

197 days ago 12:50PM, Mar 14
Lov u 2. Muahhhhhhhhhhhhhhh!!!! :)

196 days ago 1:20AM, Mar 15
Baby I'm about to come through. U up?

196 days ago 1:30AM, Mar 15
Always up 4 u. C u n a bit.

Leigh let the tears fall. She was more made at herself than anything was. She had wanted to believe in Tyrique, believe that she had finally found her own man to kick it with. She hated to admit it, but she was envious of Shia's home life. She had a man who was by her side through everything. Even now, Trent was at the hospital by her hospital bed patiently waiting for her to open her eyes, clench his hand, anything and Leigh wanted that in her life. Why is it that for some women it was so easy to find their mate and for the others they couldn't get it right to save their lives?

Closing the text messages on his phone Leigh switched over to the call log and was surprised as she scrolled through that he had Natalia listed in his call log and had spoken to her as recently as today. That little fact really peaked Leigh's curiosity. It seemed weird that Tyrique knew Shay and Natalia. Leigh understood that the world was small, but it wasn't that dag on small. This couldn't just be circumstantial.

A banging at her front door let her know that Tyrique was probably conscious and angry that she had knocked him out and taken his phone. However, he was going to have to call the police to get his property back because she wasn't letting him in under any circumstances and she meant that with every fiber in her being. To hell with him.

Chapter 16

In all things, there is a beginning and an end. Natalia took in
knowing that soon enough there would be an end to this
game. A game she had thought she'd wanted to play, but now
that she was knee deep in it, there would be no way out. She
was having a change of heart. She wanted Trent, but she didn't
take too kindly to Phylicia forcing her to do anything.

Trent was everything she'd searched for in a man and Natalia
believed in living in the moment, the game would stay the same,

but the rules had to change. She needed to be on more equal footing with Phylicia.

"I want out." Natalia said into the phone. She no longer wanted to play this game that she had started. She knew with every day that passed things were getting closer] to coming to a head and she hated to admit that she really wasn't ready to go up against Phylicia just yet.

"There is no out. This is something you started…don't make me end it."

Natalia knew Phylicia's background and knew that she meant business. However, she hadn't expected things to turn out the way that they had.

"What would it take?"

There was a pause on the other end of the line. In reality, it couldn't have been more than a couple seconds, but it felt like a lifetime.

"Death." The line went dead.

Natalia was ready to prepare for the war to take place. She had been spending the past couple of weeks bidding her time to figure out a game plan. There had to be a way to take the psycho out and she thought she had finally found one. Dialing another number Natalia waited patiently for the line to be picked up.

"Hello?"

"Shay, I don't want to do this anymore."

"Do what?"

Natalia exhaled loudly, "Everything. I should have never done the things that I did. Now there is no exit for me. I feel as if I joined a gang or something and they won't set me free."

"I plead the fifth. I know nothing about nothing." Shay replied, smiling up at Tyrique as he entered the room where she was.

"I'm sorry Shay. It's all part of the game, please forgive me."

"Huh? Forgive you for what?"

Shay had barely gotten the words out before Tyrique swiftly came up behind her and snapped her neck.

Removing the phone from her lifeless hands, he put it up to his ear.

"It's done," he said into the receiver.

"Thank you." Natalia whispered hanging up the phone.

In the bedroom at the brownstone, Natalia laid back in her bed and closed her eyes. She would have never gotten Shay involved in his scheme if she had known in combat there were always casualties of war, but she hated that Shay had to be one of those casualties. The two of them went way back to playing hopscotch on the sidewalk and chasing the ice cream truck together. Shay knew all about the things her brother did to her as a child and the constant fear that she lived in day in and day out.

"No sleeping on the job. I need a status update." Phylicia said as she whisked into the room and stood in front of Natalia's bed.

"Shay is dead," she answered in a flat tone.

"Who cares about Shay?" Phylicia said not impressed that the person driving the van during her escape was deceased, "What about Shia? That was your mission for today as well. How did that go?"

"She's still alive."

Phylicia narrowed her eyes and uncoiled the whip she had wrapped around her waist.

"Why is that?"

Natalia's eyes widened as she watched Phylicia hold the whip in her hand.

"The nurse came in an-"

The tail of the whip snaked across Natalia's lip, reopening her healing gash.

"Dammit!" Natalia screamed out.

"I gave you one job and you couldn't do that."

Natalia glared at Phylicia as she touched her tongue to the gash on her mouth and tasted her own blood, but didn't utter a word.

"So you're a mute now?" Phylicia asked, bringing the whip down across Natalia's face again. Natalia screamed out in agony.

"You can't do anything right." Phylicia said as she produced a set of handcuffs and rope from her pocket, "You're going to remain in here and think about your actions. When you're remorseful you can come out again."

Dragging the whip across Natalia's body one more time Phylicia quickly grabbed her wrist when she yelped out in pain and handcuffed her to the bed. Grabbing a hold of her feet, she bonded them together.

"See you in a couple of days, sweetie. Hopefully by then you will have a complete attitude adjustment." Phylicia said smugly leaving the room.

***

Trent opened his eyes slowly when he felt his hand being squeezed. Completely disoriented it took him a moment to realize that he was in Shia's hospital room and must have fallen asleep. Feeling his hand being squeezed again, Trent looked up at Shia's face and saw her staring back at him. He jumped to his feet as his heart began doing somersaults in his chest. The tears Trent held back all this time finally fell. He couldn't help himself; his Shia was awake.

He kissed her face all over, "Thank you for coming back to me. I love you," he whispered reluctant to leave her side, but knew that he needed to call the nurses so they could have a look at her.

"I'll be right back. I promise he told her kissing the tip of her nose. Shia blinked rapidly and sighed in relief.

Trent waited patiently in the lobby as the doctors and nurses checked Shia out. His emotions were raging out of control. He'd phoned Leigh and told her as soon as he'd left the room, so he was waiting for her to get there.

Trent broke into a smile when he saw Leigh finally coming toward him in the lobby.

"I'm so happy." Leigh said approaching Trent with a smile on her face as she bent down and kissed him on the cheek. "So, it's really true, she's awake and talking?"

"She is awake." Trent told Leigh as she sat down, "But I haven't been able to get back in and see her since I told them she was awake."

"I'm so excited." Leigh couldn't stop smiling. She needed some good news in her life after the whole Tyrique and Shay situation. This is really when she realized how much she missed having her sisterly talks with Shia, "So what are they saying?"

"That we have to wait and can see her in a little while."

"Wonderful." Leigh exclaimed, "Remi is flying up tomorrow. She's beside herself. We've been praying for so long now that it is apparent that our prayers have been working."

"Hello." The nurse said to the two as she came out of Shia's room. "You can go in and see her now."

"Trent stood and looked down at Leigh who hadn't budged. " You coming?" He asked her, "You go first." Leigh offered, "I'm sure she needs her husband's touch first."

Trent was grateful to Leigh for once. Holding his wife was a necessity. Trent entered the room slowly.

Shia watched him walk through the door and marveled at how unkept and scruffy he appeared to be. She smiled when he kissed her on the forehead then trailed his lips down to her cheek.

"Thank you," he whispered.

"For what?" Shia's voice rusty from non-use.

"For coming back to me," he closed his eyes inhaling her scent. "I need you so much. You can never leave me."

Tears escaped Shia's eyes as she swallowed past the lump in her throat.

"I'll never leave you. I promise. No matter what," she told Trent as she stared into her husband's beautiful eyes. She knew he had been worried. Trent tended to lock his emotions away deep down inside.

Trent sat in the chair next to her bed and gripped her hand for dear life.

"I missed you," he told her.

"I know you did." Shia raised her other hand to caress the side of his face, "But I'm here now."

Trent rested his face in her hand. He needed his wife's touch as he needed air to breathe. "How's my little princess?" Shia asked attempting to lighten the mood, "I know my baby has to be wondering where her momma is."

"She and the boys are down in the play area. Leigh brought them up here to see you. I'll send them in soon. I just wanted some time with you first."

Trent stood, "I'm a send Leigh in. She's been waiting."

"Okay. I love you." Shia told him as he leaned down to kiss her.

"I love you most," he told her leaving the room to fetch Leigh.

"Thank God you are alright! Honey girl you had me worried." Shia couldn't help but smile as Leigh entered with all her sassiness.

Leaning down to give and kiss, Shia Leigh plopped down in the chair next to her bed.

"Okay, yeah so this whole extended hospital stay stuff ain't hot." Leigh shook her head, "No ma'am. No more of this."

"I didn't exactly plan on ending up in here." Shia told her.

"I know, boo. How are you feeling?" Leigh asked with sympathetic eyes and a concerned tone.

"Better than I look I'm sure."

"You look good Shy. No one will even be able to tell that you were in the hospital, honestly. And your hair got longer."

"So my husband won't be repulsed. Good to know."

"Chile, please. You know better than that. Trent worships the ground that you walk on."

"He better." Shia replied cracking a smile, "So what's been going on? What have I missed?"

Leigh frowned her face up. "You up to all this, shouldn't you be resting?"

"I've been resting, over it."

Leigh laughed, "Okay. Remember Tyrique?"

"Vaguely." Shia responded.

"Vaguely is good because he turned out to be an asshole, so there's really no reason to remember him anyway."

Shia rested comfortably on her pillows, "So what happened?"

203

"He and my friend Shay were getting it on in my damn apartment. I get heated every time that I think about it."

"Girl shut your mouth! You lying?"

"If I'm lying Shy I'm flying?"

Shia giggled. Leigh could be so over the top extra sometimes.

"So what did you do?"

"Leigh grinned widely at her, "Cracked his PlayStation over his head, drug him into the hallway, threw his stuff in the hall with him, and took his cell phone." Leigh laughed.

"Lei Lei you gonna give me a heart attack. Are you serious?" Shia joined her in laughter.

"Ok, see don't joke about heart attack, because yeah, we still in the hospital and I don't want to think about that stuff." Leigh lectured her lightly, "And yes, I am very serious, but good riddance to them both. They can have one another as far as I'm concerned. I took a risk jumping out there dating again. Now I am officially done."

"Officially done, wow. Don't do that Leigh, he's out there. Give it time."

"Nah, I'm good." Leigh said not even entertaining the prospect.

The room door opened and Trent entered carrying Joelle with the twins following behind him.

Shia's eyes lit up; as Leigh moved to the side out the way to give Shia full access to her children.

***

Phylicia opened the door and stared down at a barely conscious Natalia strapped to the bed. It had been two days since she'd been in to check on her.

"You messed up." Phylicia told her, "All you had to do was the job given you. However, since you didn't, Shia made it home. She was never supposed to see that place again. You were supposed to lead Trent to me and you couldn't do that, so now I'm going to have to go to him.

Chapter 17

"Momma look!" Joelle squealed happily, as she played with her Barbie's in the middle of the family room floor. She'd brought her entire Barbie collection in the room and had them and their accessories everywhere and Shia didn't even complain about the mess, she was just happy to be there to see it.

"I see." Shia smiled down at her tiny tot.

The doorbell ringing interrupted Shia's thoughts. Leigh and Remi had run out to the mall with the boys and Trent had gone to get them food, which only left Shia and Joelle in the house, and Shia sighed as she made her way to the front door and opened it.

"Can I help you?" Shia asked the woman who had her back to the door.

"Not really, but that will change soon enough." The woman said as she turned to face Shia.

Shia's eyes grew wide and her scream was cut short as the woman punched her in the temple and she slumped to the floor. The woman smiled, it was high time for the games to begin.

When Trent arrived home, he could immediately sense that something was amiss. The house was entirely too quiet for one that housed a toddler.

Setting the bag of Thai food down on the counter in the kitchen Trent called out Shia's name. Hearing no response his heartbeat began to quicken. He hoped that she and Joelle were up in the bedroom taking a nap.

Opening his bedroom door Trent stopped walking when he was greeted by the scene inside.

"I'm so glad that you could join us." The woman smiled at him, "We've been waiting for you."

Phylicia?" Trent stared into her eyes. "What is this about?"

"You and I. Hasn't that what it has always been about?"

"No." Trent said cautiously as he kept all of his attention focused on Phylicia.

She was lying in his and Shia's bed with Shia's lingerie on. The entire room was illuminated by candles that lined the wall.

207

"It's about my family now," he continued, "Speaking of which, where are they?"

"We were a family first. You remember that?" She asked him ignoring his question.

Trent closed his eyes willing himself to remain calm.

"Phylicia, please tell me where Shia and Joelle are. Joelle is just a baby. Please don't hurt her," he pleaded.

Phylicia blinked back tears," Khloe is fine.

Trent paused, at a loss for words when he heard her mention Khloe, "P, Khloe is dead remember, you killed her."

"No, she was here when I came to the house; playing with Barbie's."

Trent shook his head, "No P that was Joelle.

Phylicia continued speaking as if she didn't hear him.

"She is so perfect. Our little Khloe. I thought she was gone, but when I came here to see you there was our baby playing in the middle of the floor. Trent she was right there." Phylicia's voice filled with awe, "She let me pick her up and hold her like I had never been gone. It was amazing."

"Okay P. Where is Khloe?" Trent asked, choosing to go along with Phylicia's warped train of thought.

"She's safe now. No one will be able to hurt her again, including me."

Trent took slow steps toward Phylicia, he felt it his heart that she wouldn't hurt him.

"Why are you here P?"

"Because I love you." Phylicia stated without hesitation.

"I know you do. But you're visiting me for a reason." Trent said in a patient tone, "What is it?"

"I want us to finally be a family. We can be parents to Khloe and raise her together."

"Phylicia, our time has passed. We tried to be together years ago remember. It didn't work out."

"But why." Phylicia asked, reentering the present, "After I told you the truth about everything, why couldn't we make it work?" She stared at him with her heart in her eyes. "I came clean about everything. If you loved me once, you can love me again."

Trent sat on the bed alongside Phylicia, "Because I have a family now. I'm sorry about all of the bad things that happened to you, but we can't live in the past, we have to live in the present and keep pushing forward. This moment right here is what's important."

"Don't you love me?"

"You will always hold a place in my heart P," he said grabbing her hand, "No one will ever take any of those memories away from us, but I have to respect my family now, the same way you would want me to respect you. Please don't hurt Shia and Joelle, they are my family now, if you hurt them, you'll be hurting me."

Phylicia blinked rapidly as the tears continued falling. "I would never hurt you again. I've always loved you. I never meant to hurt you. I didn't mean to take Khloe from you."

"I know P. However; we can make everything right now. Just tell me where Shia and Joelle are."

"Her name is Khloe!" Phylicia shouted smacking Trent across his face, "Why won't you call her by name?"

The bedroom door banged open.

"Because she's dead bitch!" Natalia yelled as she limped into the room with a gun in hand and Tyrique following behind her.

The commotion jolted Phylicia out of her altered state of mind. "You! How did you break out of that room?"

"Not because of you, now shut up!"

Phylicia looked at Natalia nonchalantly, not in the least bit worried or concerned.

"Trent; Shia and Joelle are in the nursery. Get your family and get out." Natalia told him, keeping the gun trailed on Phylicia.

Phylicia watched as Trent left the room. She was unconcerned about him she had gotten to him once. She would get to him again. Right now, she had to focus all of her attention on Natalia.

"I should have killed you at the house."

"But you didn't, did you?" Natalia said weakly. She was sure at any moment her body was going to give out from malnourishment, but she had to push through.

"To my deepest regret." Phylicia responded unconcerned.

"Go tie her down." Natalia instructed Tyrique. Tyrique took two steps toward Phylicia.

"I wouldn't do that if I were you?" Phylicia warned in a singsong voice. Tyrique kept moving toward her.

"You think I don't remember you?" Phylicia asked him. "I remember everything. The day you helped me escape was the day you got assigned a death sentence."

She shot the gun she had hidden in the blanket on the bed. The bullet connected to his throat and he fell to the ground.

Natalia's composure slipped a notch when she realized that Phylicia was armed as well and had just taken out Tyrique.

Phylicia shook her head, "You try so hard Natalia, but you never think things through. You're smarter than this. Do you honestly think I'm not prepared at all times for an attack from you?"

Natalia, still holding the gun pointing at Phylicia, had no idea what she was talking about. From where she was, standing Phylicia was the one at a disadvantage.

"Where'd you get that gun?" Natalia had her gun for years, she kept it in her nightstand at home, but she wasn't going to tell Phylicia that.

"Lemme guess," Phylicia continued talking, "Your nightstand?" She said answering her own question. "In your haste to leave the house after your little friend rescued you, did you even bother to take notice the weight of your gun is off?"

Natalia's mind zoomed in on the weapon in her hand. Now that Phylicia made that comment, she focused on the fact that her piece did feel light.

Phylicia laughed evilly from the bed. "You were so cute though. You had your little role down to a T. Nothing Oscar worthy, but still good, I'd buy a ticket to your show."

Natalia would have ran at Phylicia if she had the strength in her body, but she did not and unlike her weapon, Phylicia's was fully loaded and Natalia knew that she had no problems using it

Hearing the sirens approaching in the distance Phylicia hated that she had to forgo killing Natalia so that she could escape.

"You have a lot to learn. You should thank God because he spared you today." Phylicia said hopping out the bed and sprinting toward the windows in the bedroom.

Before Natalia could blink, Phylicia was gone. Natalia kicked herself. She hadn't thought of an escape in the event that she would need one. Now she didn't know what to do. Following Phylicia's lead, she hopped out the bedroom window as well putting as much distance between herself and the house as she possibly could.

***

Trent had never been so thankful for Natalia than he was when she entered his bedroom door holding Phylicia at gunpoint.

His family had been where she said they were in Joelle's nursery. Shia had been drugged, tied and gagged while little Joelle had only been drugged. He was thankful that his family was okay. After Shia and Joelle were discharged from the hospital, Trent knew that it was time for them to relocate. He no longer felt that he could keep them safe. He had finally agreed to let his family go into protective custody until the police could find Phylicia and bring her in.

Chapter 18

Time was of the essence. Phylicia felt like the entire world was after her and she had to take everything in stride and move quickly. The police suspected that she would be going after Trent and his family, but she had other arrangements in place. Blond wig, tanned skin, and sunglasses she resembled Storm from X-Men. The disguise afforded her the opportunity to hide in plain sight. Her target was in her view and she meant to take out her target by any means necessary.

***

Natalia felt uneasy. She'd been in Miami Beach for months hiding out from her old life and trying to blend into her new one. Today was her first day outside on the beach. She hadn't been able to take being cooped up in the boarding house she was in for another second. She had stayed inside for her own protection trying to give things with Phylicia time to cool down. She knew that Phylicia was out the somewhere and would be looking for her, which is why she had gone to great lengths to disappear. However, with the beach being full of people, how much danger could she really be in she thought as she laid her blanket on the sand to get some sun?

"Hi." Natalia glanced up as a very handsome man was looking down smiling at her. Natalia flipped over and smiled uneasily. She had just laid out on the beach and this man had popped up out of thin air.

"Hello," she replied sitting up on her blanket.

"Mind if I join you?" He asked plopping down before Natalia had a chance to decline his offer.

"I'd rather be alone if you don't mind." Natalia told him, not wanting to offend him, but not trusting anyone right now. Nervously looking around observing her surroundings, she now felt exposed.

Standing abruptly, she gathered her blanket up. Without looking back at the guy, she made her way back to her room.

Back in her room at the house, Natalia began to relax. She hated feeling uneasy because she wasn't the scared type, but not being familiar with the territory was putting her at an extreme disadvantage.

Opening her closet door Natalia reached for her bathrobe and cocked her head to the side frowning when she realized that it wasn't there. She could have sworn that she had left it hanging on the door hanger.

"Looking for this?" Natalia froze when she heard the familiar voice on the other side of her closet door. Cursing herself because she'd left her switchblade in the bag; she'd carried to the beach, which was now next to the door.

Pulling the closet door, closed Natalia faced her nemesis Phylicia. Natalia took in the blonde wig, oversized sunglasses and darkly tanned skin.

"You thought you could get away from me? I own you, did you forget?" Phylicia asked in a menacing tone. "Now sit down she ordered Natalia.

Natalia was many things, but a punk she was not; if Phylicia wanted her to do anything, she was going to have to make her Plain and simple.

"No," she told her in a firm confident tone.

"No?" Phylicia repeated, removing a small hatchet from her bag and bashed Natalia's kneecap in.

Natalia immediately dropped to the ground screaming in agony. Phylicia's face lit up like a kid at a candy store as she watched Natalia squirming around on the floor clutching her knee.

Phylicia knelt on the floor in front of her, "Now see what you made me do?" She began shaking her head, "If you had only done as I asked you to do you wouldn't be in this situation now. How does your knee feel?" She asked Natalia sweetly.

Natalia was in blinding pain, she knew her kneecap was shattered.

Phylicia stood and watched Natalia withering around on the ground like a snake.

"You know the really crazy part about this situation Natalia," Phylicia spoke while removing a knife from her bag, "I respect you. If things had been different and you hadn't set me up to take a fall so that you could have Trent; you and I would have been an amazing team. I admire your spirit and tenacity." Phylicia looked down at her, "In another life the two of us would have been friends."

Natalia snorted, "Not in any lifetime could we have been friends."

Phylicia's eyes flashed angry when she heard Natalia's comment. Sinking to her knees on the floor Phylicia grabbed Natalia's face and held it in her hands remembering her as the little girl she had met all those years ago.

"I know. I know what your brother did to you. I know all the years that he molested you and you felt like you had no one to turn to. I understand being angry with me for not stepping in to help. You thought as his wife I should have saved you, right?"

217

Phylicia felt the hot moisture flowing from her eyes. "And maybe I would have been able to if I had been able to save myself. However, I couldn't save either of us. He helped make me this way."

"You did nothing to help me and then you took Trent from me."

Phylicia let her face go and stared at her as if she were delusional. "I didn't know you were dating Trent. You were holding on to a grudge for no good reason. I didn't know about you. Trent came after me. You should have put on your big girl panties and let it go like any mature woman would have."

"You were married to my brother!" Natalia spat at her, "I thought you would have had the decency to respect your marriage."

"You know what kind of monster Maxwell was. There was no love lost there."

"You're both monsters!"

"Yeah?" Phylicia stared at her, "And what about you? Stop trying to be the innocent here. You're not."

"I am the innocent. Maxwell raped me for *all* my teenage years. You don't get over things like that, you just don't."

"You're preaching to the choir Natalia. You're my sister in law and I love you, but I can't forgive you for what you did to me. That is the ultimate betrayal and I'm done discussing this with you." Raising her hand quickly Natalia jabbed the knife's blade into the center of Natalia's throat and cut all the way down to her collarbone, Blood splattered on Phylicia's face as she made the cut. Pushing the blade in further she retraced the gash she'd made with the blade. Removing the knife from Natalia's flesh, Phylicia wiped it off on the blanket Natalia had with her on the beach; she wiped off her face as well, grabbed her bag, and left the room as silently as she had come.

***

"Baby you need anything? Trent smiled in Shia's direction. He was so happy to have his wife up and busying herself around the house again, that he didn't know what to do.

Shia returned his smile, "No. I am good babe. Thanks for checking on me though." Shia said from her place on their sofa. Trent had been so attentive to her and she was loving all of the extra attention lately.

Trent walked up to her and drew her in close for a hug. "I love you," he said placing a kiss on the top of her head."

"I love you too with your sexy self. She said laughing as she tapped his nose with her finger.

Trent laughed as he nipped at her finger. He absolutely adored his wife.

"I may have some news for you later, so stay tuned."

"Will do." Trent laughed as he left her on the sofa in peace, so that he could begin the family's dinner for the evening.

219

Epilogue

Watching them act as a family unit at the park, Phylicia was sickened to her stomach. This should have been her family. She should have been the one with Trent playing with children as they ran around. However, unfortunately, she was not and if she had her way, Shia wouldn't either. Dropping her Caramel Apple Spice in disbelief when Shia turned in her direction and Phylicia got a good look at her, she couldn't believe her eyes at the size of Shia's belly. *Along comes baby number two.* She thought, but she'd be damned if there would be another. Rising from the table she started in their direction; a gun with a silencer in her bag it was time for the puppets to see that the Puppetmaster truly was the one that made them dance.

About the Author

A native of the Metropolitan of Washington, DC, Mychea has had a dream to have her words shown in print since the age of eleven, when she began a series of illustrations and short stories. In April 2007, Mychea decided it was time to stop fantasizing and begin achieving, opting to turn her dreams into a reality and so her debut novel Coveted began.

She is the author of urban fiction novels He Loves Me, He Loves You Not 1 & 2, Coveted and Vengeance and Playwright of her stage play He Loves Me, He Loves You Not, and Coveted. In her spare time, Mychea loves to draw, model, and act and plan events. She is hard at work on her next novel and stage play. You can view more about the author at www.mychea.com.

Books by Good2Go Authors on Our Bookshelf

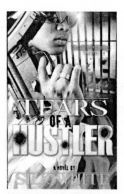

Good2Go Films Presents

To order books, please fill out the order form below:
To order films please go to www.good2gofilms.com

Name: _____
Address: _____
City: _____ State: _____ Zip Code: _____
Phone: _____
Email: _____
Method of Payment: ☐ Check ☐ VISA ☐ MASTERCARD
Credit Card#: _____
Name as it appears on card: _____
Signature: _____

Item Name	Price	Qty	Amount
48 Hours to Die – Silk White	$14.99		
He Loves Me, He Loves You Not - Mychea	$14.99		
He Loves Me, He Loves You Not 2 - Mychea	$14.99		
He Loves Me, He Loves You Not 3 - Mychea	$14.99		
Married To Da Streets – Silk White	$14.99		
My Boyfriend's Wife - Mychea	$14.99		
Never Be The Same – Silk White	$14.99		
Stranded – Silk White	$14.99		
Slumped – Jason Brent	$14.99		
Tears of a Hustler - Silk White	$14.99		
Tears of a Hustler 2 - Silk White	$14.99		
Tears of a Hustler 3 - Silk White	$14.99		
Tears of a Hustler 4- Silk White	$14.99		
Tears of a Hustler 5 – Silk White	$14.99		
Tears of a Hustler 6 – Silk White	$14.99		
The Panty Ripper - Reality Way	$14.99		
The Teflon Queen – Silk White	$14.99		
The Teflon Queen 2 – Silk White	$14.99		
The Teflon Queen – 3 – Silk White	$14.99		
The Teflon Queen 4 – Silk White	$14.99		
Time Is Money - Silk White	$14.99		
Young Goonz – Reality Way	$14.99		
Subtotal:			
Tax:			
Shipping (Free) U.S. Media Mail:			
Total:			

Make Checks Payable To: Good2Go Publishing
7311 W Glass Lane, Laveen, AZ 85339

CPSIA information can be obtained at www.ICGtesting.com
Printed in the USA
LVOW07s0856300815

452090LV00001B/198/P